Rena asked, "Mad Dog and his gang—will they be back?"

Fargo folded his arms across his chest, watching her from shrewd eyes. Finally he twitched his shoulders. "How long is a piece of string? If they think you witnessed the murders, hell yes, they'll be back."

"And you, Mr. Fargo?" she pressed, baiting him with her smile. "What are your plans?"

Fargo turned that problem back and forth for a full minute.

"I've got bodies to bury," he replied. "And since I knew Matt, I won't be leaving until those killers are put down like the rabid curs they are."

THE
TRAILSMAN
#304

DEATH VALLEY
DEMONS

by

Jon Sharpe

A SIGNET BOOK

SIGNET
Published by New American Library, a division of
Penguin Group (USA) Inc., 375 Hudson Street,
New York, New York 10014, USA
Penguin Group (Canada), 90 Eglinton Avenue East, Suite 700, Toronto,
Ontario M4P 2Y3, Canada (a division of Pearson Penguin Canada Inc.)
Penguin Books Ltd., 80 Strand, London WC2R 0RL, England
Penguin Ireland, 25 St. Stephen's Green, Dublin 2,
Ireland (a division of Penguin Books Ltd.)
Penguin Group (Australia), 250 Camberwell Road, Camberwell, Victoria 3124,
Australia (a division of Pearson Australia Group Pty. Ltd.)
Penguin Books India Pvt. Ltd., 11 Community Centre, Panchsheel Park,
New Delhi - 110 017, India
Penguin Group (NZ), cnr Airborne and Rosedale Roads, Albany,
Auckland 1310, New Zealand (a division of Pearson New Zealand Ltd.)
Penguin Books (South Africa) (Pty.) Ltd., 24 Sturdee Avenue,
Rosebank, Johannesburg 2196, South Africa

Penguin Books Ltd., Registered Offices:
80 Strand, London WC2R 0RL, England

First published by Signet, an imprint of New American Library,
a division of Penguin Group (USA) Inc.

First Printing, February 2007
10 9 8 7 6 5 4 3 2 1

The first chapter of this book previously appeared in *Terror Trackdown*, the three
hundred third volume in this series.

Copyright © Penguin Group (USA) Inc., 2007
All rights reserved

 REGISTERED TRADEMARK—MARCA REGISTRADA

Printed in the United States of America

PUBLISHER'S NOTE
This is a work of fiction. Names, characters, places, and incidents either are the
product of the author's imagination or are used fictitiously, and any resemblance
to actual persons, living or dead, business establishments, events, or locales is
entirely coincidental.
    The publisher does not have any control over and does not assume any respon-
sibility for author or third-party Web sites or their content.

The Trailsman

Beginnings . . . they bend the tree and they mark the man. Skye Fargo was born when he was eighteen. Terror was his midwife, vengeance his first cry. Killing spawned Skye Fargo, ruthless, cold-blooded murder. Out of the acrid smoke of gunpowder still hanging in the air, he rose, cried out a promise never forgotten.

The Trailsman they began to call him all across the West: searcher, scout, hunter, the man who could see where others only looked, his skills for hire but not his soul, the man who lived each day to the fullest, yet trailed each tomorrow. Skye Fargo, the Trailsman, the seeker who could take the wildness of a land and the wanting of a woman and make them his own.

Death Valley, California, 1861—where a beautiful woman's treachery is as deadly as an evil man's bullets.

1

Skye Fargo heard the screams from a half mile off, the high-pitched, almost feminine screams of a man who was suffering the worst hurt in the world. Fargo recognized the sound and knew it was pointless to charge recklessly forward—the poor soul was past all help.

The Trailsman, as some called Fargo, gigged his black-and-white pinto stallion forward, lake blue eyes ever vigilant in the brittle afternoon sunlight and furnace heat. He was traversing the upper end of California's Death Valley, bearing toward Grapevine Canyon, which led down from the bleak and jagged mountains. Even down low in the dry creek wash he was following, winds whipped billows of sand, salt, and grit into his face and eyes.

More piercing, scalp-tingling screams from ahead raised the fine hairs on Fargo's arms. His nervous Ovaro whiplashed his head.

"Steady, old campaigner," Fargo calmed him, patting his neck. "He's about to go over the mountains, and we might, too, if we get careless."

Fargo was crop-bearded and wore fringed buckskin shirt and trousers, a tall, broad-shouldered man cut down to puny size by the sheer vastness of this sterile, 150-mile-long trough. Death Valley was walled by rock outcrops and surrounded on all sides by eastern California's merciless desert.

Fargo had only to climb a little higher, however, for a magnificent view of the Sierra Nevadas and their capes of dazzling white snow. But even a naked woman couldn't have distracted him from the horrific screams as he rode around a hill of black slag and two bodies eased into view.

The bridle-wise Ovaro stopped when Fargo tossed the reins forward. He swung his right foot over the cantle and landed light as a cat, sliding his brass-framed Henry from its boot. Fargo's sun-slitted eyes searched the rock-salt bed of the valley, but nothing moved except a few wisps of white-gauze cloud far overhead. There was nothing there that *might* move, for very little life existed in this wasteland.

"Aww, *Jee*-zus, it hurts!" screeched the one man who still clung to life. "Aww, God, it's pure fire!"

Both men had gotten in front of a bullet, the dead man a shot through the heart, the screamer a bullet low in the guts—even in cities with doctors a gutshot was fatal, much less out here in the most arid, barren region of the West. Each man had been shot at such close range his shirt caught on fire from the powder burn.

"Mister," begged the dying man when he spotted Fargo. He was a young man with an honest face. "I know I'm dead. But, God A'mighty, some water first."

"Sure wish I could do more, friend."

Fargo laid his Henry down and twisted the cap off his bull's-eye canteen. It was dangerously low, but Fargo couldn't deny even a dying man a drink.

"Who did this?" he asked as he knelt and cupped the man's head so he could drink.

Somewhere amid a string of curses and screams Fargo heard the curious words "mad dog." The dying man, his face contorted with pain, clutched the Trailsman's sleeve.

"Woman!" he gasped. "She's . . . next. Killers . . . Christ-o*mighty* that hurts! Mister, *please* pop one in me."

Fargo could stand it no longer. Every instinct in him wanted to save life, not take it, but this suffering man could last for hours, with each minute like a year in hell. His weapon was missing, so Fargo shucked out his Colt and set it near the man's hand. Only seconds after he started to walk away, the weapon spoke its piece.

"I hope I helped you," Fargo muttered, tasting the bile of sudden anger as he returned for his revolver. No skunk-bit son of a bitch was making him play God like this and just riding off into the sunset.

Fargo searched both men and found letters written by Allan Pinkerton, the Chicago detective, identifying them

as two operatives in his employ. That bothered Fargo—
Pinkerton men were generally brave and capable.

A woman . . . she's next . . .

Fargo flinched hard when a gunshot split the lifeless silence, coming from Grapevine Canyon. He sprinted toward his stallion, even as two more shots echoed down the long valley known as Death.

Rena Collins felt fear hammering at her temples, but she tried to balance her conflicting impulses, knowing that one tiny mistake now meant brutal rape and death.

"What do you want from me, Mad Dog?" demanded Matt Conway, the silver-haired gent who had given Rena shelter only an hour earlier after her guards were brutally slain.

"Innocent as a nursery, ain't you?" replied one of the meanest-looking men Rena had ever seen. "Did you think you could railroad Mad Dog Barton's kid brother to the gallows and live to brag about it?"

"Railroad? Christ sakes, your brother, Lanny, murdered a woman and her four-year-old daughter."

Rena, cowering in the loft of a small cabin, watched the brute's mouth curl into a sneer. "He did, didn't he?" Mad Dog said proudly. "That boy was hell on two sticks."

Rena gasped at this callow man, but Scotty McDaniels, the aging prospector who had saved her from Mad Dog and his gang, touched her arm in warning. His upper right thigh still oozed blood from a bullet one of the gang had put in it.

"Yessiree, Deputy Conway," Mad Dog went on. "You kill one of mine, I kill *all* of yours."

"Now, simmer down. I retired last year. Hell, I didn't kill your brother. I only brought him in for trial."

Mad Dog wore a richly embroidered sash with a pair of ivory-hilted, silver-mounted revolvers stuck into it. But he also held a shotgun, and Rena felt her skin crawl against her clothing when he thumbed back both hammers with a loud metallic *snick*.

"You *only* brought him in, Conway? Just a little Judas kiss, eh?"

Mad Dog's face, Rena realized with a violent shudder,

lived up to his sick name. His eyes, cunning and primitive, were two flat yellow disks, and when he talked or grinned, his lips pulled back to reveal teeth narrow and pointed like fangs.

Two more men had forced their way into the cabin with him, a small, furtive Mexican wearing rope sandals and a redheaded man whose hands were taking shocking liberties with Matt Conway's spinster daughter.

Mad Dog glanced around the cabin. It was simple but solid, with a puncheon floor, sawbuck kitchen table, and cast-iron cookstove. The one touch of elegance was a mirror in a bronze frame on the back wall. Rena flinched when Mad Dog drew his belt gun in a blur of speed and shot the mirror to shards.

"The first family living in Death Valley," Mad Dog sneered. "Thought you'd be safe here, uh?"

Scotty again touched Rena in warning. His weather-seamed face looked white as a fish belly beneath his iron gray beard and mustache.

"Mad Dog, what's the point of this?" Conway tried to reason with him. "After all, your brother—"

"*I'm* the cock of this dung heap, not you. First you leave my brother dancing on air, now you stand there and piss in my boots. That's no way to treat a man, 'specially when he's got you behind the eight ball."

"At least *please* leave my wife and daughter out of this!"

Mad Dog shook his shaggy head. "Can't be did, law dog."

"Please!" Conway repeated, his tone passionately earnest. "Don't punish them for my actions!"

"You mean, like this?"

Mad Dog swiveled toward Conway's wife and tweaked the gun's right trigger, the report deafening in the small cabin. The heavy buckshot cut Marsha Conway nearly in two and blew gobbets of bloody flesh all over her husband.

The retired deputy loosed a bray of grief, and the effort not to scream left a pinch in Rena's throat. Hearing the terrible pain in Conway's voice, she felt the saline sting of tears.

"Please," the shattered man begged when Mad Dog pointed his double-ten at Conway's shocked-numb daughter. "Not her, Mad Dog. *Please.*"

4

"My side hurts from laughing so hard, starpacker. You're gonna watch it, you shitheel *honest man*, and you're gonna see it forever in hell, printed on the back of your eyelids. This is for Lanny."

The prospector beside Rena carried a black-gripped Remington six-shooter tucked into his belt. She aimed an entreating gaze at it, but he shook his head in silent frustration.

"There's three below and one outside," he whispered. "They'll kill us both."

This time Mad Dog aimed deliberately high, nearly decapitating the Conway girl. The color ebbed from Rena's face as the horror of what she was watching sank in deep.

Matt Conway fell, sobbing, to the floor, driven mad by what he'd seen. Mad Dog finished him off with six bullets.

"The daughter's still warm," the redhead said. "Let's fetch the Kid inside so he can get him a poke. He likes it when they cooperate."

An unbidden noise of disgust in Rena's throat made all three men stare up toward the shadowy loft. She and Scotty were already pouring sweat from the stifling heat, but now it flowed like snowmelt.

"I think we just found our fine-haired sketchin' woman," Mad Dog announced. "And this one ain't goin' to waste before we kill her."

Yellow eyes gleaming with malice, a faint smile twitching one corner of his mouth, he headed toward the ladder.

Scotty had his six-shooter to hand now, ready to make his last stand. Rena's pulse leaped into her throat, and she eased a derringer from the pocket of her skirt. It was only a single shot, and she knew full well that lone bullet had her name on it.

"Heads up, boys!" a voice shouted from outside. "Rider comin' in loaded for bear!"

Rena, on the verge of firing a bullet through her right temple, heard a rapid drumbeat of hooves and felt hope soar within like the brush of wing tips against her heart.

"It's only one," the redhead scoffed. "We can snuff his wick easy."

"Good odds," Mad Dog agreed. "But if he gets away, he'll ride out of the valley now before we can stop him. Won't be long before the whole state knows who butchered the Conways. A tin star they might ignore, but not two women."

"I take your drift," the redhead said. "If we leave the cabin first, ain't nobody can get out of this valley without us knowing it. Besides, the Kid ain't no sharpshooter, and this hombre might kill our mounts."

"Now you're whistlin'. We give him no chance to escape. Let's hop our horses and get out of here before this hombre sees us. Kid!"

"Yo!" shouted the voice outside.

"You're hid good in that pile of scree. Stay there and watch this jasper. Then pull foot and meet us at the usual place."

Rena, realizing all three men were racing to their horses, sagged to the floor, trembling too hard to stand up. The rider was so close now she could hear his bit ring rattling.

"Whoever this man is, Mr. McDaniels," Rena told the prospector, "he just saved our lives."

The prospector, gun in hand, peeked out through a break in the chinking. "Too soon to tack up bunting, miss. The one who just rode up looks like he could fight a cougar with a shoe, and he don't strike me as the type to let laws get in his way."

2

As he galloped the Ovaro farther into Grapevine Canyon, Fargo felt his jaw drop open in astonishment. Someone had built a ramshackle cabin on the salt-encrusted bed of the canyon. Fargo had spotted a few abandoned prospectors' shacks in the Death Valley region, but this was a real dwelling—true, the mud chinks had baked to dust, and hastily notched logs made the place lean, but it boasted glass windows and a stone chimney.

He saw no more signs of human life as he drew back on the reins, slowing his stallion to a trot and cautiously studying the barren surroundings. A slope-off roof on the east side of the cabin sheltered a buggy and a pair of big bay horses.

"Hallo, the cabin!" he shouted. "Permission to ride in!"

"Draw rein right now, slick!" replied a gravelly voice from within. "I ain't no killer, but I *will* shoot you if you come closer!"

Fargo did as told. "Say, lower the hammer. I heard gunshots and came to take a look."

"Who are you?" the voice demanded.

"The name's Skye Fargo."

"The fellow called the Trailsman?"

"That would be me."

There was a harsh bark of scorn. "Whoopie doodle! And I'm John the Baptist."

"You're not exactly a play-the-crowd man, are you?" Fargo said sarcastically. "Look, is everything all right in there?"

"Hell no! Three decent people are lyin' on the floor, dead as a can of corned beef—two of 'em women. And, mister, you're in range of a killer hidden close by to watch this place. He's prob'ly notching his sights on you right now."

Before Fargo could react to the warning, a rifle cracked like green wood. The first bullet kicked up a geyser of rock-salt only inches from the Ovaro's forelegs; the second fluttered past Fargo's head and whined on down the valley, chased by its own echo.

Fargo was adept at the science of survival and made his calculations instantly. For the moment his hidden enemy held the whip hand, so Fargo jerked his feet free of the stirrups and rolled out of his saddle on the off side, keeping the pinto between him and the shooter.

He knew his horse was a giveaway target, so he led the nervous Ovaro behind the shelter of the cabin. He dropped low and waited at one corner, the merciless desert sun hot enough to peel the hide off a Gila monster.

The dry-gulcher fired again, and this time Fargo's frontier-trained eyes spotted a blue curl of smoke above a large pile of scree. He threw the Henry into his shoulder socket, worked the lever, and opened fire, peppering the position.

He glimpsed a man wearing a floppy-brimmed hat and butternut-dyed homespun. The figure disappeared behind a basalt turret, and then Fargo heard iron-shod hooves ringing on hardpan as he escaped.

A portly man in his late fifties, wearing the ore-stained clothes of a miner, waited outside when Fargo rounded the front corner.

"Mister, maybe you *are* the Trailsman," he said as he greeted Fargo. "I'd swear you was *smilin'* when you rolled off that saddle."

"I'm used to killers trying to free my soul." Fargo glanced at the dried blood on the man's leg. "Looks like you got in front of a bullet, Mr. . . . ?"

"McDaniels, Scotty McDaniels. I was a hog reeve back in Memphis before I pulled up stakes and headed west to the Comstock. But there's too damn many men there in Virginia City, packed in tight like maggots in cheese. So I pointed my bridle toward California. I cannot abide bein' close-herded."

Fargo nodded approval. Most men tacked into the prevailing wind, but he liked to chart his own course, and evidently Scotty McDaniels was of a like mind.

Fargo said, "A man after my own heart. You say there's dead inside—"

Fargo fell silent when a striking young woman in her early twenties stepped outside into the broiling sun, a woman trying to project haughtiness to cover her shock and fear. She was a strawberry blonde, medium height and slender, with her hair pulled back in a braided coil at the nape and a full-lipped, rosebud mouth.

"Miss Rena Collins, Mr. Skye Fargo," Scotty mumbled, rusty at the social graces.

"Thank you for coming when you did, Mr. Fargo," she told him in a stilted tone as if he were a servant. "You saved our lives by scaring away the killers."

Fargo took in the side-lacing ankle shoes, blue broadcloth skirt, and white shirtwaist amply swollen in the bodice.

"I can tell," she added, her tone combative, "from the way you look at me, that you believe any woman traveling out here must be a strumpet."

"You're insulting the intelligence of strumpets, Miss Collins. They aren't stupid enough to waste their time—or lives—in this hellhole. Do you even know where you are?"

"In a place that's hardly even been charted," she retorted. "Death Valley. It earned that grim name twelve years ago when twenty-seven wagons, carrying a hundred souls, stumbled onto the place by accident. Only one wagon made it out."

Fargo was impressed. "Sounds like you know plenty."

"I'd ought to. My older sister and her husband were among the dead who gave this vale its name."

"I'm sorry for your loss," Fargo told her, "but what's the sense of coming to join them?"

Red splotches of anger flared in her cheeks, and she frowned in tight-lipped indignation. Before she could reply, however, Fargo stepped inside the cabin.

"I never seen the like in all my born days, Mr. Fargo," Scotty said, limping in behind him. "It's the devil's own work."

Fargo smelled it immediately: the sheared-metal odor of blood. Three bodies lay slumped on the floor, the two females horribly mutilated by close-range shotgun blasts—one nearly ripped in two, the other almost decapitated.

The sight rocked Fargo back on his heels, and his muscles went warm and weak with anger. The man was spitted through with bullets, but Fargo immediately felt a shock of recognition.

"Matt Conway," he said. "A former U.S. deputy marshal. The women must be his wife, Marsha, and his daughter, Juliet. I never met 'em—until now."

"So you knew him," Scotty said.

Fargo nodded. "Peace officers earn less than chimney sweeps, and Matt had to take extra work to support his family. Me and him freighted cookstoves into the Sierras during the gold rush. He was a good man."

"Hunh, don't I know it. He gave me and the ice princess out there shelter after the killers done for her guards."

"These guards," Fargo said, "were they Pinkertons—two of them?"

"There was two, all right, but that's all I know. I just met the woman mebbe an hour ago. Mr. Fargo?"

"Yeah?"

"Why in blazes would Conway settle in Death Valley? Ain't even a shitsplat of a town anywheres near here, and him with two women."

"That's a stumper," Fargo admitted. "Actually, this spot isn't in the valley—Grapevine Canyon has water. Matt jugged plenty of vicious owlhoots in his time. Prob'ly wanted to protect his women."

"That shines," the wounded prospector agreed. "One of the killers said he was avengin' a brother Conway sent to the gallows."

Fargo had more questions on that score, but the sight on the floor taxed even the Trailsman's strength.

"Just *damn*," he said softly before turning on his heel and walking back outside.

The woman was returning to the cabin from a pile of moraine about a hundred yards distant. She rode a chestnut gelding with a blazed forehead and a white mane. A swayback mule trotted reluctantly behind her on a lead line.

Fargo's numb sadness was already slow-boiling toward anger. As he waited for Rena, he cast his eye southward at the vast desert trough few men could survive. Hot, dry, lonely, desolate—Fargo doubted there was anyplace like it in the world. This was July, and summer temperatures in Death Valley reached a suffocating 134 degrees in the shade.

He had not spotted one blade of grass when he crossed the heart of the valley two days earlier. Just flat, parched earth stretching between walls of sterile mountains, with not a speck of vegetation. Water holes were scarce and well hidden, many of them salt-encrusted ponds with cheery names like Badwater.

"What the *hell* are you doing out here?" Fargo demanded as Rena rode up to the cabin. "There's two dead women inside, and a total of five people dead, counting your guards. Lady, you're mighty easy to look at, all right, but you must be soft between your head handles."

"I *watched* those women die, Mr. Fargo," she retorted as she swung down and hitched her gelding to a pole supporting the slope-off. "And my two guards a little earlier. As to why I'm here . . ."

She took a folding canvas camp stool and an artist's sketch pad from a big saddle pannier and sat down in the scant shade of the cabin, working quickly and efficiently with a nubbin of charcoal.

"My father publishes *Frontier Scenes Magazine*," she explained as she rapidly drew a face with lupine features. "I was sent out here from Boston to sketch Death Valley in all of its dimensions. In fact, I was sketching the Funeral Mountains when I was attacked."

Scotty joined them, favoring his injured leg.

"Your sister and brother-in-law died here," Fargo told her, "and you've come out here to sketch the place for a pleasure magazine? Sent by the same father who's lost one daughter out here already, no less. Sorry, that's thin."

She was sternly pretty when she frowned. "You call ladies liars, Mr. Fargo?"

"Not even when they are, Miss Collins." Fargo chuckled in spite of his queasy feeling that this woman would become serious trouble.

"Say, that's a good likeness of Mad Dog," Scotty chimed in as Rena finished shading in deep-set, hooded eyes.

Both men stared over her shoulders in fascination as her slim white hand finished the rapid but impressive sketch.

"Mad Dog," Fargo repeated. "The dying Pinkerton man spoke that name. The handle's new to me, but not the pan—that's a cockroach named John Barton. He and his kid brother, Lanny, ramrodded a road gang around Los Angeles. Matt collared Lanny a while back, and he ended up decorating a cottonwood."

"Yup, that's the jasper, all right," Scotty said. "He mentioned his brother by name, Lanny. This here Mad Dog packs a pair of fancy revolvers, but he's no two-gun punk."

Fargo studied the picture, almost feeling those long fangs in his skin. "Well, now it's done, they can stick or quit. Barton's heap big trouble if he sticks. No matter what gang of cutthroats he rides with, he's always the biggest toad in the puddle. He'd kill a nun for her gold tooth."

"That's a keen insight into the obvious," Rena said with a regal tilt to her chin. She closed the pad and rose from her canvas stool. "We just watched him prove his ruthlessness, Mr. Fargo. Your 'colorful' speech hardly matches the real images."

"No need to get on the peck, Miss Collins," Scotty interceded. "Mr. Fargo is a frontiersman, and that class of men ain't much for talkin' like books."

"Never mind," Fargo said. "She's windy, but she's right. Scotty, siddown with your back to the cabin. If that wound isn't treated it could mortify."

Fargo first brought the Ovaro around front, hobbled him, and gave him several hatfuls of water from a barrel beside the door.

"Need a horse?" Fargo asked Scotty as he used his Arkansas toothpick to cut away denim cloth. "There's two good ones here."

"Nah. General Washington is a good mule. Me 'n' horses don't get too chummy."

"We'll liberate them, then," Fargo decided. "The valley's only twenty miles wide, with water holes past the mountains. They'll smell water."

"You'll find a bottle of old orchard in my saddle pocket," Scotty said. "Mind if I nip before you poke around in that bullet hole? And go easy with that frog sticker—I got no more britches."

Fargo got the whiskey and handed it to him. He stared,

astounded, as the itinerant sourdough took the level down by four inches.

"You're not just drinking, old roadster," Fargo marveled. "You're a pipe through the ground. Go easy in this heat."

Scotty corked the bottle and smacked his lips. "When it comes to good whiskey, better to go down hard than to hedge. Care for a snort? It ain't bad corn juice if you put your fist through a wall to help it down."

Fargo passed, knowing how alcohol dehydrated a man in the desert. He probed the bullet hole carefully with a hoof pick. If it hurt, Scotty was too drunk to care.

"The bullet's small caliber," Fargo reported, "but it's in pretty deep. I could cut it out, but you'll likely bleed to death—this air sucks blood up like a sponge. So let's just leave it in. I'm carrying two bullets and a flint arrow point myself."

"Hell, cut the whole damn leg off," Scotty invited. "It's stove up with rheumatic anyhow. Matter fact, cut 'em *both* off and call me Shorty."

"I'm a good Samaritan, not a surgeon."

Fargo washed the wound in carbolic he carried in his saddle, then wrapped it with linen cloth that Rena provided.

"He was really quite brave," she told Fargo. "The men who killed my guards were about to seize me when Mr. McDaniels opened fire on them, scaring them off. Then he led me to the Conway cabin. Little did we realize this Mad Dog Barton and his gang would show up there."

"A-huh, *that* was the squaw that stroked the camel's sac," said drunken Scotty, a pun so bawdy that Rena pretended she hadn't heard it.

"The killers didn't know you were at the cabin?" Fargo asked her.

Rena shook her head. "I don't think so. Not until I made a noise from the loft. Thank God they heard you coming and panicked at the idea of being seen."

"Leg feels fine," Scotty announced.

" 'Limb,' " Rena primly corrected him.

"I never learnt any parlor manners," the graybeard said apologetically.

"How many in this gang?" Fargo asked, feeling his sweat evaporate the moment it appeared in the dry air.

"Three in the house," Rena said, "and one outside they called Kid. He's the one who shot at you."

"The other two," Scotty supplied, "was a Mexer who kept his face buttoned up and a redhead with a two-gun rig. That Mex—I don't think all his biscuits're done."

"I knew it would not all be beer and skittles out here," Rena mused aloud, "but I never expected *this*. I filtered my expectations through longing, not logic."

"That's too far north for me," Fargo said impatiently. "Never mind the stage talk. Do you have any plan for getting out of here?"

His brusque tone made her rosebud mouth flatten in a frown. "When I'm *ready* to leave, I will go to Mission San Fernando, about thirty miles northwest of the pueblo of Los Angeles. It is an inn and a stagecoach stop."

Fargo shook his head in amazement. "Such stupidity is refreshing. This is no place for spoiled daddy's girls."

A shadow of apprehension moved across her pretty face. "Are you going to *force* me to leave?"

"Why does that prospect turn you white as chalk?"

"It's just . . . I'm not finished yet," she faltered out. "With my work, I mean."

"You're poor shakes as a liar," Fargo said. "Nobody's willing to die just to make some sketches. But no, I won't force you to leave. People have a right to be stupid."

Relief softened her features. "Mad Dog and his gang— will they be back?"

Fargo folded his arms over his chest, watching her from shrewd eyes. Finally he twitched his shoulders. "How long is a piece of string? If they think you witnessed the murders, hell yes, they'll be back."

"And you, Mr. Fargo?" she pressed, baiting him with her smile. "What are your plans?"

Fargo turned that problem back and forth for a full minute.

"I've got bodies to bury," he finally replied. "And since I knew Matt, I won't be leaving until those killers are put down like the rabid curs they are."

3

Fargo grained and watered Conway's horses. Two hard slaps and a gunshot sent the bay geldings into the wild.

"Shouldn't we have kept them?" Rena asked.

"Not enough grain and water for four horses and a mule," Fargo replied, his eyes closed to slits as he studied their harsh surroundings.

"Mr. Fargo—"

"I prefer Skye. Most folks who call me mister are after my money."

"After your money?" A skeptical dimple wrinkled her fair cheek. "Mr.—I mean, Skye—my family was among the first Beacon Hill Bostonians. My people had money in the days when it was still called wampum out here."

"So did mine," Scotty cut in, joining them in the shade under the slope-off roof. "We stole it from your family."

He was still drunk as Davy's saw, but nonetheless her haughty manner was back. "No doubt. That's what happens when men lack moral training and large-scale ambitions."

She looked at Fargo again. He held his Henry rifle in his right hand as he watched for their enemies.

"Skye, why on earth are *you* out here?" she asked.

"They need hunters bad around Virginia City to provide fresh meat for the miners. A few days' work will stake me for months. I picked the Death Valley route to avoid the mountains. I helped the army map this area, and I know where to find water."

"You know the area?" she repeated, suddenly very interested.

Fargo's mouth quirked, not quite in a grin. "Why's that so important?"

Rena realized she'd been indiscreet and tried to look bored. "It's not. I just thought it might be useful as I search for places I want to sketch and paint."

"Sure," Fargo said from a deadpan. "Sketch and paint. Is that all?"

"Of course. You see, I'm here to record images in places too wild for the new photography. To provide an artistic and spiritual element that the realism of photography cannot capture."

"Artistic and spiritual," Scotty repeated, his tone ridiculing the words.

"A noble venture," Fargo conceded. "But a dangerous one, too, especially for a woman alone."

Those ruby red lips pursed seductively. "I'm not alone now. And you said you weren't leaving until you track down the killers."

"Ahh . . ." Fargo waved her words off impatiently. "Look, you and Scotty managed to jump over a snake this time. But in terrain like this, luck won't go too far. We need to get you out, and until we can you need to lay low."

"Where? Here in this cabin?"

Fargo shook his head as he pulled the shovel off Scotty's mule. "Too conspicuous. Right now we're at the upper edge of the valley. I don't like this canyon. Too many ambush points. We'll have a better chance in the valley itself—it's flat and wide open. But we'll worry about all that later. Right now there's graves to dig."

Fargo hated to do it, but he buried all three Conways in a single shallow grave—the slightest labor, in this unrelenting desert heat, made a man light-headed.

"Mount up," he told the other two when he'd finished. "Those Pinkertons can't draw buzzards out here, but we can't just leave them, and we need to stick together."

They rode down from the mouth of Grapevine Canyon onto the desolate, sand-blown plain of the valley floor. The long trough of Death Valley ran north and south; to the east and west there was nothing but spectacular jumbles of rock walls with very few breaks. Even here, however, Fargo's frontier eyes could find beauty. The colors of the mountains changed frequently as the sun struck the rocks at different angles, and a valley completely devoid of vegetation was oddly striking.

However, he spent most of his time watching for riders. Scotty, still drunk, edged his mule closer to Fargo.

"Skye," he muttered, "I might be gettin' snow on the roof, but I'm still a bull in the hot moons. That Rena would make a gelding feel like a stud, hey?"

"Pipe down, you old letch. She'll hear you."

"Just look how she's riding like a man," Scotty said persistently. "Young feller, there's no way, no how, a young gal can get her quim rubbed like that fir hours and not get in rut."

"Bottle it," Fargo snapped.

"Like hell I will! Too bad you come along—ol' Scotty coulda been dippin' into the jam pot come dark."

Fargo snorted. "That's a hoot. Hell, I ain't close-herding her, you old fart. I say she'll give you the frosty mitt, but don't let me stop you."

"Me? I never plant my carrot, gamble, nor drink," Scotty informed him piously. He winked and added, "Whilst I'm prayin', that is."

"Why would anyone plant a carrot?" Rena demanded, overhearing him but failing to understand.

"Manner of speaking," Scotty mumbled, suddenly sober.

Rena gigged her chestnut up beside Fargo. "Any sign of Mad Dog and his gang?"

Fargo shook his head. "Tracking won't be easy in the valley. Some of this bed is solid rock, and what sand or salt there is gets blown around constantly in the winds."

"Then how will you know where they are?"

Fargo pointed to a mile-high rocky pinnacle in the barren Black Mountains. "That's called Dante's View. You can see most of Death Valley from up there."

A minute later they reached the two bodies and swung down, hobbling their mounts. To spare Scotty's wounded leg, Fargo dug the grave by himself, another shallow single hole for both Pinkertons. He was forced to rest in the shade of his Ovaro after he finished.

"We can't stay exposed to this sun and heat by day," he told his companions. "But we can't wander too far from Grapevine Canyon, either. There's good water there, at Furnace Creek, and it's the only place I know of where our horses can tank up quick."

17

When Rena lifted her canteen to drink, Fargo stayed her hand.

"Water's going to be scarce and it must be hoarded," he warned her. "Don't drink in the sun—it'll just evaporate from your pores before you get the use of it."

"But I'm thirsty!"

Fargo thumbed a cartridge out of his gun belt and handed it to her. "Pop this in your mouth and suck on it like candy. It'll cut down on your need to drink."

"Don't chew on it," Scotty warned from a deadpan, "or you might shoot your mouth off."

Her glacial stare made it clear she had no interest in bad puns.

"Let's tote up our food," Fargo suggested as they prepared to mount. "I've got pemmican, coffee, a bit of cornmeal."

"I've got buffalo jerky, salt pork, and hardtack with some weevils in it," Scotty reported. "And whiskey."

"All my provisions were in the guards' saddlebags," Rena lamented.

"Their horses were likely stolen," Fargo said. "Well, there's no game down here. I do know a spot where we can catch saltwater sardines, and there's mesquite in the canyon—the pods are good food."

Rena looked aghast. "Saltwater sardines? Oh, my cornucopia runneth over."

"Never mind," Fargo said, helping her into the saddle. "Looks like you two are with me, and I'm going nowhere until I figure out if the killers have left. Let's all go look for our new home."

Ten miles south of Grapevine Canyon, tucked into a seam in the west wall of the valley beneath the Panamint Mountains, a few rotting timbers marked the headframe of an abandoned mine. The Busted Flat had produced good color in the 1840s, but the ore abruptly turned to solid bedrock in '53. Its location was hidden from travelers on the valley floor, and the abandoned shaft stayed cooler than the desert outside. It was also large enough to accommodate horses.

"I rode off," George "Kid" Papenhagen explained to

Barton and the others, "but this hombre in buckskins never chased me. So I snuck back afoot."

Despite being over thirty, Papenhagen answered only to "Kid." Mad Dog Barton would have shot the strutting peacock by now if it weren't for his skill with locks and safes. He was a shirker and a coward, but handy with a revolver and rifle and eager to kill when the risk to him was low.

"The skirt set up her little stool," Kid went on, "and commenced to sketch, with the bearded jasper studyin' on it close."

"What was the drawing?" demanded Taffy Thomas, the redheaded Welshman.

"Hell, I was over fifty yards out, you lunkhead. But it sure's hell wasn't no nature paintin'."

"This could be trouble, boys," Mad Dog said, cautioning all of them. "If I'd been sure somebody was in the loft, I'd've killed her before we vamoosed. The thing is, I wanted us the hell outta there before we was spotted."

Three members of the gang sat around a burning kerosene lamp. The fourth, Pepe Lopez, stood guard outside the entrance.

Mad Dog suddenly cursed, lips pulling away from his long yellow teeth. "That high-hatting bitch *had* to witness the rubout of Conway and his family, and good chance she's at least got my face on paper. Likely, she'll draw all of you, too."

He looked at Papenhagen. "Kid, you say this rider had a beard and wore buckskins?"

Papenhagen nodded.

"Big man?"

"Big enough. No fat, all muscle and sinew."

Mad Dog's yellow eyes went distant and brooding. "He didn't ride a black-and-white pinto stallion, did he?"

"Christ yes! You know him?"

"Know of him. His name's Skye Fargo. Some call him the Trailsman."

"Un hombre peligroso," Pepe called from up front, where he could hear every word amplified by the shaft.

"Damn straight he's a dangerous man," Mad Dog confirmed. "He's the crusader type, and the Conway rubout is right up his alley."

19

"So? No skin off my ass," Taffy said. "Plenty of dangerous men out west, and I've sent several to their ancestors."

He drew a .36 Colt Navy to make his point. The grips bristled with tacks, one for each kill. Taffy had fled to America after raping the wife of a schoolteacher in his native Wales. The redhead had since become a murderer, arsonist, road agent, and, like Mad Dog, a master of draw-shoot killing.

"We'll settle Fargo's hash," Mad Dog agreed. "But we'll have to be careful with him. He's shiftier than a creased buck."

"You and Taffy won't even need to clean your guns," Kid Papenhagen scoffed. "I'll curl the Trailsman's toes."

Mad Dog and Taffy exchanged looks and burst into mocking laughter.

"Kid," Mad Dog said, "you couldn't fill a straight if it was open at both ends. Skye Fargo is tough as a two-bit steak. He earned that Trailsman moniker by always knowing where the high ground and the escape trails are. As to gunfightin'—he'd drop you like a sack of dirt."

"Like hell he would!" Papenhagen bristled. "You boys're gettin' me mixed up with Pepe. Them chilipeps got no cojones for a cartridge session. That's how come they prefer to flash knives."

"Chinga tu madre," Lopez called from the entrance. He was small, quiet, and unfriendly, and Mad Dog had never seen him without his black flat-crowned sombrero with its rattlesnake band. Only average with firearms, he was deadly up to seventy-five feet with a throwing dagger. One was hidden in each of his stitched-calfskin boots.

"Unpucker your assholes, both of you," Mad Dog growled. "We're not leaving Death Valley until every witness to the murders is dead. From now on we keep track of them night and day and make sure they don't go to law. As for Fargo—he ain't an eyewitness, but he'll likely protect them. So we *will* row that bastard up Salt River."

The sun sank lower and the shadows purpled and flattened out. Fargo led his charges along the east wall of Death Valley, hidden from view by the scree and moraine from the sterile mountains. The dry heat sucked the moisture from their eyeballs and forced them to blink sparingly or risk irritating their eyes.

Fargo was looking for a safe place to camp. The lack of animal predators made the job easier, but two-legged beasts posed worse threats.

Rena's chestnut bridled when it almost stepped on a pile of sand-obscured human bones.

"That hunk of weathered metal in his right hand was a gun," Scotty said, "and it's aimed at the skull. I guess it's true—many a man stranded out here has cashed in his own chips."

Fargo watched Rena sigh melodramatically. *"Sic transit gloria mundi,"* she quoted solemnly.

"Huh?" Scotty said.

"Oh, nothing."

"Lady," opined the prospector, who was in a scratchy mood now that his drunk had worn off, "your wick is flickering."

"Go to hell!" she blazed, nostrils flaring.

Fargo gave that a hoot. "Look around you. We're already there."

"Never mind her jabberin'," Scotty said. "Seems like she's always got sand in her ointment."

Rena gave both of them a snide smile. Even when she played the ice princess, Fargo noticed, she got him stiff in the saddle. Hot-tempered women were explosive in the heat of carnal passion.

"Can't we just roll our blankets on the ground behind these rock tumbles?" Scotty asked, his mouth so dry the words were slurred.

"We'll do that if we have to," Fargo said. "But I remember a four-man prospectors' shack somewhere along here. If we get jumped, I'd prefer to be behind walls."

Rena, Fargo noticed, spent all her time searching the desolate mountains rising above them. At one point she directed Fargo's eye to a sandstone formation.

"Would you call that a bottleneck shape?" she asked him.

The place she pointed out was just to the right of a gap in the Funeral Mountains that gave egress into Death Valley.

"Could be," he replied.

"May we go up there?"

"Lady," Scotty broke in, "have you been smokin' the Chinee pipe? Take us two hours to climb up there in this

21

blazin' heat. And for what? You can draw it from down below."

"Mind your own business," she reproached him. "I hardly think a down-at-the-heels itinerant can make artistic judgments."

"What you're searching for," Fargo suggested, playing a hunch, "isn't inspiration."

"You're calling me a liar?" she demanded.

"Let's just say you're detouring the facts."

"I get it." She bit the words off in anger. "Saving me was a noble gesture—at first. But already the shoe is pinching, right? Since it's me they want, you're looking for any feeble excuse to desert me."

"Hoo-doggie!" Scotty exclaimed. "She pinned your ears back, buckskin boy."

"Let me guess," Fargo told her. "Your daddy spared the rod?"

The mirth bled from Scotty's face, and he fixed a steel-eyed stare on Rena. "Before you start rockin' the boat, m'heart, you best take the temperature of the water. Right now four owlhoots hard as sacked salt are out to kill you, and me and Skye are all you got."

4

Twice, as Fargo scouted the mountainous east wall of Death Valley, the heat forced him to slacken his saddle so the Ovaro could take in more air. A bloodred sun was finally on the verge of dropping below the horizon, and in the desert, sunset meant welcome relief—as much as forty degrees cooler.

"Where the hell's this old shack, Skye?" Scotty McDaniels demanded, busy gnawing on a hunk of salt pork. "Be dark soon."

Fargo ignored him, watching the Ovaro's ears prick yet again. Something was disturbing the stallion, and in a place this lifeless "something" was almost surely men.

"You dodgasted churn-head!" Scotty fumed when his mule tried to burst forward in a run. "General Washington must smell the water ahead in Grapevine Canyon."

"Could be," Fargo said. "But he might've whiffed a mare, too. You know how mules are partial to their company."

The moment Fargo fell silent, General Washington loosed a raucous bray and bolted forward, almost throwing Scotty from the saddle. Neither the prospector's curses nor his sharp tugs on the reins could stop the mule's headlong rush.

"Like I feared," Fargo told Rena, "it's a mare."

Her tired face tensed. "Mad Dog and his gang?"

"Seems like a safe wager. This valley isn't exactly crawling with people."

Fargo unbuckled his heavy leather gun belt and handed it to her. "You and your horse stay behind the rocks. Can you load and fire a six-gun?"

She nodded. Her chestnut, too, seemed skittish, so Fargo quickly swung down and removed his rarely used picket pin. He led the chestnut behind black volcanic boulders and stomped the picket pin into the hard ground with his heel. He knotted the end of the reins, buried it deeper with the pin, and stomped the earth around it.

"Wait!" Rena protested as he got horsed again. "I'll be here all alone!"

"That old salt saved your life today," Fargo reminded her. "Now *he's* all alone."

"But . . . what if you don't come back? What will I do?"

"The time to worry, princess, was *before* you came this far west."

"Skye Fargo, how dare you—"

But the Trailsman gave her a careless wave, thumped the Ovaro with his boot heels, and they bolted forward toward the mouth of Grapevine Canyon.

Out ahead, Scotty was being tossed in the saddle as General Washington continued his headlong run despite the heat. He suspected Fargo was right about mares in the canyon, but leaping out of the saddle was not an option. Not only could he ill afford the loss of his mule and equipment in this desert region, but his bones were old and brittle—a leap onto solid bedrock, at this speed, could easily break his neck.

"The gods have pissed on me all my life," the old prospector groaned, wishing he could at least break out some corn juice and die drunk.

General Washington entered the mouth of the canyon, sped past the Conway cabin with its new grave, and threaded his way through a scattering of huge boulders. Just ahead was a thin trickle of Sierra runoff known as Furnace Creek. It formed a small pool where horses could drink one at a time. And sure enough, four men were gathered there in the waning light, weapons trained on Scotty as he flashed into view.

A white mare that had caused this mess was just then drinking, the Mexican in the flattop sombrero holding her. Scotty also spotted two horses the red-handed murderers had stolen earlier from the guards they killed. He knew he had seen his last sunrise—these four jackals were raised from birth to eat six-shooters.

"By the boot!" Mad Dog Barton exclaimed as General Washington stopped so suddenly Scotty almost flew over the pommel. "What have we here, boys? Looks like the old fart's attacking us!"

"Nah. His jenny smelled Pepe's mare," Kid Papenhagen said.

Mad Dog's lips eased back. "You're goin' up, Methuselah, bank on it. But first we have us some fun. Taffy, his beard's a mite scruffy. 'Member how we trimmed the whiskers of that mouthy preacher out in Pikes Peak country?"

"Sure do," Thomas replied, hauling Scotty roughly out of the saddle. "There's a powder flask in my right saddlebag."

When Scotty struggled, Mad Dog clipped him in the temple with one of the fancy ivory-and-silver guns in his sash. The men stretched him out on the ground and sprinkled his beard with black powder. Scotty screamed like a banshee when Papenhagen struck a phosphor to life and dropped it on his beard, igniting a fizzling hell of sparks and heat and pain.

When the four owlhoots finally quit laughing, Mad Dog said, "Stand up and strip buck, old codger."

Scotty sat up, still groaning from the burns on his face. "Strip? The hell for?"

"You're gonna shinny up a tree, old man."

At first Scotty could make no sense of it. He'd never seen one tree in the Death Valley region. This, however, was a slightly less arid canyon, and when he glanced around him, his bowels went loose and heavy with fear.

Several honey locust trees grew near the water, trunks covered with needle-sharp thorns between an inch and eight inches in length.

"I ain't climbin' no honey locust," Scotty told them. "No way in hell."

"It's a shooting point with us," the redheaded Welshman called Taffy informed him. Kid Papenhagen drew one of his .44 Army pistols, 1860 model, and thumb-cocked it.

"Kiss my lily-white ass," Scotty retorted. "Might's well just go ahead and plug me."

"Start with his oysters," Mad Dog said, and Papenhagen shoved the gun into Scotty's crotch.

He screamed blue murder when a gun went off, but the

louder scream was torn from Papenhagen when a bullet from Fargo's Henry chewed into his forearm. The bullets kept chunking in, sending the gang behind rocks with their mounts.

Scotty required no invitation to save his own hide. This time General Washington responded to his master when Scotty vaulted into the saddle and raced toward the mouth of Grapevine Canyon.

Once again the Henry's 16-shot magazine ruled the day as Fargo pinned the men long enough for the old salt to ride clear. He had an excellent position in a basalt turret overlooking Furnace Creek.

"Any of you boys want the balance of these pills," he invited them in a shout, "don't be bashful!"

"Fargo, I'll perforate your liver, you lanky son of a bitch!" Mad Dog roared back.

So far nobody was shooting back, and Fargo grinned when he realized why—no one knew where he was. Guessing that they would hunker down for a while, unsure, he climbed back down to his horse and followed Scotty's retreating form back into the flat, low valley.

"Skye, 'pears like that's twice you've saved me," Scotty told Fargo after the sun went down. "In *one* day! Happens I survive this hellhole, I'm lightin' a shuck back to the Comstock."

"You and I are upset, Scotty." Rena spoke up in the moonlit dimness of their rude camp in the rocks. "But notice how calm Skye is. Violence seems mundane to him."

Fargo didn't miss her goading tone. Nor did he mind it— women who liked to snoot him, he'd noticed in his travels, were the same ones who tore their clothes off in a frenzy and climbed all over him in search of naughty pleasure.

"Calm goes with bein' determined," Scotty told her. "And with stayin' alive out here."

Working in scant light, Fargo ran a metal-toothed currycomb over the Ovaro, spending the longest time on the witch's bridles, tangles in the mane.

"Well, *eating* goes with staying alive, too," Fargo reminded both of them. "I spent my day pulling you two out of the fire, so I figure one of you should feed me cooked rations. We can chance a small fire behind these boulders."

"Don't look at me." Rena protested from her perch on the canvas camp stool. "We have seven servants in my family, not counting the dailies."

"A woman who can't cook," Fargo roweled her, "is like a man who can't handle horses."

"Do you really care about a woman's cooking," she teased back, "if she's the right kind of woman in the heat of passion?"

"Almost all of them are the right kind then," Fargo opined.

"No differences?"

She couldn't see his face at this distance, but he grinned anyway. "Oh, a few stand out."

"If you're thinking I'll try to make that elite list," she replied in reproach, "it won't happen. I believe strongly in social subordination, and my class must not . . . mingle intimately with yours."

"Judas Priest," Scotty muttered in disgust at her arch tone and manner. "What's it like to be ten inches taller than God? Lass, we spanked the king of England on his ass and tossed him out before I was born."

"I'm still hungry," Fargo reminded them mildly.

"I don't cotton to wage labor," Scotty said, "but I like to cook. I'll do it. Thing is, I ain't no great shakes at it."

Fargo scooped out a small fire pit and lined it with crumbled bark and dry sticks kept in his saddle pockets. "Ash pone is good enough. Then I'll boil some coffee."

"You two are brave, but you're surely easy to please," Rena barbed.

"It's fine by me," Fargo told her, "if you prefer soft-handed men who need stores so they don't starve and go naked. But they don't last long beyond the settlements. Out here, ash pone and coffee is a feast."

"I'm grateful to have it," she admitted reluctantly.

"Hallelujah," Scotty muttered as he formed balls of cornmeal and water.

"But when," Rena pressed, "will we find this cabin?"

"Shack," Fargo corrected. "If it's still there, we'll find it tomorrow."

Rena sighed histrionically. " 'Mere man—his days are numbered. Whatever he may do, it is but wind.' "

"Plenty of wind around her, all right," Scotty muttered,

and Fargo burst out laughing. He finished currycombing his stallion and moved to the fire.

"Show me a gal who talks like a book," Scotty said in Fargo's ear, "and I'll show you the town—"

"What was that, Mr. McDaniels?" Rena demanded. "Some more coarse filth, I'd expect."

"I reckon we can't all be scrubbed angels like you, m'heart."

"I never claimed I was sinless," she snapped. "Or that I don't enjoy . . . pleasures of the flesh." The fire showed she was clearly staring at Fargo when she added, "But I'm careful what kind of man I select."

"Why?" Scotty demanded. "All cats look alike in the dark."

"Maybe she likes to do it during daylight," Fargo chimed in. "You get to see more that way."

"At my age," Scotty said with a woebegone smile, "dark is best."

"I see you've *both* kissed the Blarney stone," she said dismissively.

After supper Fargo and Scotty decided to stand guard two hours on, two hours off. The three of them unrolled their groundsheets and blankets, Rena seeking privacy within a tight circle of tall boulders.

"Just curious," Fargo told her while he softened her bed ground with his Arkansas toothpick. "Why all the interest earlier in climbing up to that bottleneck shape?"

"I thought it might make a good composition."

Fargo watched her in the moonlight as she unbuttoned the top button of her shirtwaist. "That's thin. You're lying about who you are and why you're here."

She undid the next button, watching his face closely. "I know what you're thinking, Skye. You're picturing me naked."

"So? What a man's thinking is none of your picnic."

A third button popped open. "Think—and stare—all you want. It will never happen unless you . . . outrage me."

Fargo gave that a chuckle and stood up, brushing salt dust off his knees. "My girls are all volunteers."

"And there's been *plenty* of volunteers, I'm sure."

Fargo shrugged. "Who counts? Women are like

stagecoaches—if you miss one, another will be arriving soon."

He was about to step outside her circle of boulders when she said in a throaty tone, "Even so, some rides are smoother than others."

Her tune had abruptly changed, but Fargo didn't mind. "Doesn't sound like you're trying too hard to discourage me," he pointed out.

"Sometimes I feel like volunteering," she replied. "I'll be here all night."

Fargo gave each of the horses and Scotty's mule several hatfuls of water from the gutbag he always hauled with him in desert country.

"Somethin' queer about that gal," Scotty remarked. He tapped his right temple in the dying light of the fire. "Room for rent, if you catch my drift?"

"Her think-piece is all right," Fargo gainsaid. "But she's up to something, no question. No way in hell would a man send his daughter into country like this to get sketches."

Fargo was too discreet to mention the latest piece of evidence: Only moments after telling him she'd never submit to him—he'd have to rape her—she invited him into her bedroll for the giddy dance. That was the behavior of a scheming woman who made her plans on the fly.

Scotty passed him a bottle. "Care for a nip?"

Fargo drank, shuddering at the sudden fire in his belly. "Jesus, old son! This liquor would make a rabbit fight a bulldog."

"That's why I drink it. Dutch courage is better than none."

"I'll take first watch," Fargo told Scotty. "Owlhoots are lazy by nature, and I doubt they'll prowl too much after dark. But go easy on that firewater."

Fargo had already cleaned and oiled his Henry. He moved out onto the open valley floor, buffeted by the cooler nighttime wind.

I'll be here all night. Rena's throaty invitation played on his mind for the next two hours, at times forcing him to adjust himself so he could walk. The thought of her creamy-lotion skin, those ripe-fruit lips, and her swollen bodice made it difficult to focus on the night and the still, lifeless valley where killers lurked even now.

He woke Scotty and sent him out a good distance.

"Skye?" Rena's voice called from within her boudoir of boulders. "I can't sleep. Come exhaust me."

Fargo knew she had ulterior motives, but as long as a woman was above the age of consent and below the age of indifference, he didn't worry about the finer points. When he stepped inside the circle of boulders and spotted her in the moonlight, hot blood surged into his staff.

"I've been waiting for you," she pouted, tossing the blanket aside.

The strawberry blond hair was loose now, a tangle of silken curls that cascaded over her shoulders. She wasn't wearing a stitch, and as Fargo stared she spread both long, shapely legs wide apart. Fargo could have sworn he felt the moist heat of her arousal from where he stood. Her breasts were heavy and full, yet rode high, ending in dark, pointy nipples.

He propped his Henry within reach and dropped his gun belt, then opened his straining fly. He knelt between her legs and she used both hands to grip him.

"*Every*thing's bigger out west," she marveled, sending tickling heat into his shaft and groin when she began stroking him. "And you're so hard and throbbing! Let's take care of the immediate pressure so the second one lasts longer."

She bade Fargo lie down beside her, her fine hair tickling his belly as she took just the tip of his manhood past those heart-shaped lips. He moaned encouragement and squirmed with pleasure as she swirled her talented tongue around the sensitive, purple-swollen dome of his manhood.

"It's big as a doorknob," she praised when she backed off to lick the shaft itself, giving little tease bites to the underside.

She used one hand to cup his sac and gently squeeze and release. Fargo reciprocated by sliding a hand between her supple thighs and gliding it up the satin-smooth skin to her wet, furry nest. Her pearl was swollen with aroused blood, and he flicked it gently but rapidly with a fingertip, firing repeated climaxes that made her gasp and shudder. His other hand played with her nipples, teasing them stiff.

Soon her inner thighs were slick with arousal, and Rena got to work on his curved saber with single-minded abandon. Like a steam piston her head bobbed up and down, and now and then she raked her eyeteeth along the underside of his length, goading him to an exploding release that bowed his entire body.

"You stallion!" she cried out a minute later when she discovered he had remained erect even after his release. She rolled onto her back and spread her legs wide, drawing her knees back. "Mount me!"

"Times like this, I like a bossy woman."

However, just as Fargo rose to his knees, several nearby gunshots shattered the quiet night, followed by a bloodcurdling yell that seemed to betoken the end of the world.

5

Fargo didn't waste time buckling on his cartridge belt. He snatched his Colt from the holster, then grabbed his Henry and raced out into the open valley. He expected to find Scotty locked in mortal combat with Mad Dog Barton and his gang. Instead, he found the old prospector staggering around with a whiskey bottle in one hand, his black-gripped six-shooter in the other.

"You old fool," Fargo snarled, grabbing gun and bottle from Scotty's hands. "You're s'posed to be on guard duty, not enjoying a hoisting session and howling like a timber wolf."

"Tarnation! No need to get all wrathy."

"Like hell!" Fargo fired back. "Thanks to your shenanigans we might have a frolic coming."

"That's why I was practicin'—shootin' pop-shots from the hip."

It required an effort for Fargo not to put a boot up the old fool's sitter. "Never mind wasting bullets on target practice. Shooting at oyster cans ain't quite the same as shooting at a man who fires back."

"These was rocks, not oyster—"

"Shut pan and get back to camp. I'll take over now."

"I got good reason fir gettin' all jollified," Scotty insisted. "Good friend of mine was kilt today."

"Who?" a skeptical Fargo demanded.

"My beard. We been trailin' together nigh onto thirty years. It looks like burnt weeds now."

Fargo never could hold a petty grudge very long. He felt himself relenting a bit. "Well, that makes a little sense," he agreed, fondly rubbing his own cropped beard. "But just grow it back—don't get all of us killed."

"Ahh . . ."

"And *don't*," Fargo added as the prospector began trudging drunkenly back to camp, "be drinking tarantula juice on guard duty."

"Mebbe I'll get me some poon from Little Miss Rich Bitch," Scotty slurred, angling toward Rena's bedroom of boulders.

Fargo grinned wickedly in the darkness. "You do that."

Scotty stumbled into the circle of boulders. Moments later a high-pitched feminine scream was followed by a slap so loud that Fargo winced. Scotty came flying out like a cannonball and staggered to his bedroll, collapsing. The snoring began almost immediately, a wheezing racket like a leaky bellows.

Fargo knew that all the surrounding mountains would mask the approach of riders at night by eliminating their skyline. He stretched out flat on the hard bed of Death Valley, using his entire body to detect the motion of horses. Nothing so far.

"Skye?" Rena's nervous voice called out. "Land sakes, what happened?"

"Scotty got on a spree and started shooting at the moon. Go to sleep. Looks like I'll be out here a while."

Fargo poured out the contents of the bottle in his hand and returned to camp. He found four more full bottles of liquor in Scotty's packsaddle. He emptied out all but one, transferring it to his own saddlebag. Then he returned for a long stint of guard duty. Only when he was sure Scotty had slept it off did Fargo finally wake him up for sentry duty and get a few hours of badly needed sleep.

Fargo never slept past sunrise except in a hotel, and then only rarely. The dull, leaden light of dawn found him brewing coffee and baking ash pone. Scotty, nursing a headache, stayed out front—no doubt to avoid Rena.

"Good morning," she greeted Fargo, looking quite fetching in a wrinkled but clean anchor-print dress of cobalt blue.

She fished a ball of baked cornmeal from the ashes and dunked it into the coffee Fargo handed her.

"Are you going after the gang today?" Rena asked.

"We need a safe location to stay in first," Fargo replied.

"Then I have to find out where they're holed up."

"How? This valley is narrow, but it's awfully long."

"Dante's View," Fargo reminded her. "That mile-high pinnacle I pointed out to you. It'll be a tough climb, but there's no choice—hoofprints barely register on this salt hardpan, and the constant wind sweeps them away."

"Since we'll be climbing so high anyway," she said, trying too hard to sound casual, "any problem if we explore that bottleneck formation?"

The stare Fargo aimed at her made Rena shift her gaze from him. "What?" she demanded. "Did I step on a corn?"

Fargo laughed and shook his head. This woman had little reverence but plenty of guile. Between her and that drunken sot of a prospector, he didn't much like the odds for his survival.

"Tell the truth and shame the devil," he told her. "Ever heard that saying?"

Last night's interrupted romp in her bedroll had not taken an ounce of vinegar out of Rena. Her look knifed him.

"Since you're so convinced I'm a criminal," she fumed, "at least tell me my crime."

"I never said you were a criminal," he said, correcting her. He flipped the dregs of his coffee into the sand and stood up. "I said you were a liar. I might believe that a father would send his daughter to Omaha or even Santa Fe to paint and sketch. But not to Death Valley. Besides, the only thing I've seen you sketch is Mad Dog Barton."

"And wasn't it well executed?"

Fargo nodded. "You're some pumpkins, all right. But I've met plenty of women who can draw—they learn it to pass the time out here. You're after something else."

"You really believe that?"

"To the marrow of my bones," Fargo assured her.

Her nostrils flared. "You're a despot." She threw the words at him. "But you're deceptively calm about it. It's placid despotism."

Fargo nodded agreement. "I tend to push people around—politely. But out on the frontier one man must always be in charge. That's what has caused so much trouble on the Oregon Trail—few men will submit to leadership. You can't put it to a vote every time the trail forks."

"Well . . . I *do* admire a take-charge man," she admitted, giving Fargo a seductive up-and-under smile that coaxed a chuckle from him. What she couldn't gain by wit and wile she'd go after with sex—a lure that usually worked with Fargo.

Scotty, refusing to meet either of their gazes after his medicine show last night, ventured into camp for coffee.

"You look a little peaked," Fargo roweled him. " 'S'matter, Romeo, did you fall off the balcony?"

"Ahh . . ."

"No need to avoid my eyes, Scotty," Rena told the sourdough. "You're forgiven for last night—after all, you *did* save my life yesterday."

Fargo gave the horses and Scotty's mule a little water and began tacking the Ovaro, trying not to dwell on the infuriating images of the Conway family slaughtered in their own home.

Neither Rena nor Scotty knew how sharp the Trailsman's hearing was. Although they were a stone's throw away from him, he heard their conversation perfectly.

Rena said, "You recognized Skye's name yesterday and called him the Trailsman. I don't understand—is he famous?"

Scotty shrugged a shoulder. "Not igzacly, I don't s'pose. But he's got him a reputation in some parts of the West."

"For what?"

"Well, they say he champions the weak but won't let himself be put upon—not by anybody."

"Is he law-abiding?" she persisted.

Scotty watched her, puzzled by the question. "He's no plaster saint, and he's jumped out his share of bedroom windows just ahead of a buckshot load. But he can hit a dime edge-on with rifle or short gun, and I hear he's sent his fair share of owlhoots to the farther side of Jordan. But he obeys the important laws, I reckon. Why do you care?"

"Just curious," she said evasively.

"Like hell you are," Fargo muttered to himself.

This gal, he told himself as he tightened the cinches, *might be a hot little firecracker in the blankets, but she's also going to be a ton of trouble. Deadly trouble.*

35

They scoured their few utensils in the salt-encrusted sand and moved on. The trio had been riding along the east wall of Death Valley, heading south, for almost an hour before the sun cleared the Funeral Mountains and began baking the barren valley floor. Fargo kept his eyes peeled for the shack and Mad Dog Barton's gang.

"Rena," he said, pointing across the salt flats toward the bleak and jagged mountains to the west. "What is that distant range called?"

"The Panamints," she replied promptly. "With the Funeral Mountains just above us. They turn into the Black Mountains a little distance ahead."

"It's no big secret about the Death Valley Party," Fargo mused aloud. "And you say you lost a sister in that group, so naturally you've read about it. But almost all of this eastern California desert is still uncharted—only a few hundred men, at most, know the official names of mountains and terrain features. Why and how would you know this area so well?"

"How can I draw something I can't name? My father sent for U.S. Army topographical maps."

Maps Fargo helped make. A wry smile divided his shadowed face. "That's real dedication to your art."

Those luscious red lips pressed into a grim straight line. "I'll have you know—"

"Stow it," Fargo said, sick of her deceptions but in no mood to argue. "Just kidding you along."

Every now and then Fargo rode back behind the tumbles of scree and moraine, searching for the shack he remembered from years earlier.

"Maybe it's gone," Rena suggested.

"Not likely," Fargo replied. "Desert air preserves wood, and there's no weather to speak of. I doubt if ten people set foot into this valley in a year's time. The Conways appear to be the first permanent residents, and they were in Grapevine Canyon, not the valley."

"Mad Dog Barton's gang 'pear to know the area," Scotty said.

"True, but don't forget that John Barton and his gang have worked the Los Angeles area for years. This is an ideal place for owlhoots on the dodge."

"Well," Scotty opined, reaching into a saddle pannier,

"Barton is the wheelhorse of the gang. If we can curl his toes, the rest—God A'mighty! Who the hell boosted my corn juice?"

"You got one bottle left, you old mash vat, and you can have a belt tonight," Fargo replied. "I'm damned if you're going to get all of us planted with your drunken jags."

"Hell 'n' furies, Fargo!" the old-timer protested. "Every man needs to cut the wolf loose now and then!"

"No sense arguing with Skye," Rena cut in. "He's a despot."

Scotty raised six sorts of hell, but Fargo ignored him, carefully watching the flat, treeless terrain for signs of any riders or a place where they might be holed up. He missed seeing the usual desert animals: coyotes, bobcats, kangaroo rats, desert foxes. He spotted no lizards darting from rock to shade nor even the long-eared jackrabbits that covered parched terrain at an astonishing clip. Fargo knew there were some desert rodents that lived their entire lives without drinking a single drop of water. But, requiring food, even they avoided Death Valley.

The trio rode past a spot that seemed familiar to Fargo. He ducked behind a virtual wall of black rock.

"Found it," he called out to Scotty and Rena.

They joined him in a well-screened pocket behind the rocks. A good-size shack with a tin-pipe chimney and windows of oiled paper—now cracked and dry—stood almost against the mountain wall.

Fargo threw the reins forward and swung down, walking to the pressed hide that served as a door. Inside, only layers of sand suggested abandonment. A small Sibley stove for cooking filled one corner, and crossed-stick shelves held pans and pottery dishes. Each wall contained a bed of canvas webbing, and a trestle table sat in the center of the rammed-earth floor.

"Good location," Fargo told the others. "Unless the Barton gang knows it's here, which I doubt, they won't find it unless they spot us coming or going."

"So what?" grumped Scotty, still miffed about his whiskey. "We don't know where the hell they are, either."

"That's our next item of business," Fargo assured him as he tipped the table to shake off an inch of salt and sand. "I plan to head up to Dante's View today."

"May I go with you?" Rena spoke up eagerly. "It should be perfect for a panoramic view of Death Valley."

"Panoramic," Scotty repeated scornfully. "The Mexers call this valley *la cola del mundo*—the tail end of the world."

"Sure, you can go," Fargo told her, watching her from shrewd, lake blue eyes. "We'll be passing that bottleneck you seem so interested in."

She pretended not to notice Fargo's skeptical tone.

"Soon as we haul our gear inside," Fargo went on, "we're heading back to Grapevine Canyon. The animals need to tank up good, and we need to fill our canteens and gutbag."

Scotty made a quick pass around the shack and returned with an oak war club bristling with spikes.

"Found it out back," he explained. "Injin, ain't it?"

Fargo nodded. "Could be Yaqui or Mohave."

"Well, seein's how you don't want me shootin' off my six-gun," Scotty said resentfully, "I'll keep this under my bunk."

The three of them rode north toward Grapevine Canyon and Furnace Creek, the dry morning air sucking the moisture out of them. Fargo again spotted no sign of any other riders.

"Maybe they rode back to Los Angeles," Rena suggested, watching his eyes scour the bleak, heat-shimmering landscape.

"It's possible," he replied. "But when women are murdered, no gang is going to leave a witness. By now it's likely they figured out you and Scotty were hiding in the Conway cabin. That guard likely heard you when you challenged me yesterday."

The three were perhaps fifteen minutes from the mouth of the canyon when Fargo spotted white plumes to the west—riders approaching.

"I'd guess they haven't seen us yet," Fargo told his companions. "Sun's in their eyes, and that white glare should be blinding them. No point in running. You two head into the canyon and water your mounts."

"What about you?" Rena demanded.

Fargo's smile was grim. "They play their games, I play mine."

38

Rena and Scotty rode toward the canyon while Fargo reined in his Ovaro and swung down. A veteran of many skirmishes in open plains, Fargo had trained his stallion to lie flat and form a living breastwork. He hooked an arm around the pinto's neck and tugged him down.

Fargo stretched out behind the Ovaro and laid his Henry across a flank.

"Easy, old warhorse," Fargo soothed when the desert hardpan began to burn and the stallion whickered in complaint. "I feel it, too."

Fargo carried field glasses in a saddlebag, but he knew better than to use them now—reflections would give him away. The riders—he finally counted four—were visible as a rippling haze, and the intense salt glare made his eyes tremble. Finally he could just make out a white horse, but not the rider.

The horse is innocent, Fargo thought as he drew a bead, *but not the rider.*

Hating to do it, but with two lives to protect, Fargo slowly took up the trigger slack. The Henry kicked into his shoulder, brass shell casing skittering across the hard desert floor. The white horse collapsed in midstride, and Fargo made out the shape of a rider flying head over handcart.

The rest paused only long enough to pick him up before reversing course and escaping to the east.

Fargo took no pleasure in shooting the horse, but at least he had turned the Barton gang away from Grapevine Canyon. However, he had made one serious miscalculation: He had forgotten that he was close to the canyon, with some snakes and lizards that occasionally ventured out onto the valley floor.

Fargo heard the warning buzz too late as he pushed to his feet. Stinging fire erupted in his left calf, and even as he skinned back his Colt and shot the pit viper, Fargo's mind warned him urgently: *Desert rattlers are the most deadly.*

6

Fargo vaulted into the saddle and ki-yied the Ovaro up to a canter, unwilling to risk a gallop or run in this blast-furnace heat. He passed the mouth of the canyon, trying not to look at the cabin where three decent people had been slaughtered, and made toward the upper plateau where Furnace Creek formed its modest pool. He saw Scotty standing guard while Rena's chestnut tanked up.

"Didja pop one of 'em over?" Scotty demanded eagerly.

"Worse—I had to kill a horse. I turned the gang, but I got snakebit in the leg."

"Good place," Scotty said, pulling the Arkansas tooth-pick from Fargo's boot. "We can fetch that pizen if we hurry."

Fargo swung down from the saddle, aware that his heart had begun racing in the past few minutes and his breathing was rapid and shallow. He slid up his trousers leg and lay down on his side in the hot sand and gravel.

"Your buckskins helped keep the bite shallow," Scotty observed as he made two stinging cuts, in the shape of a cross, on the puncture wounds.

Rena almost gasped when Scotty began sucking the blood-and-venom mixture oozing from Fargo, spitting it out to go after more.

"If his ass was snakebit," Scotty assured her, "I'm 'fraid Skye would soon be hunting the white buffalo on the big reservation. I got my limits."

Scotty rinsed the wound in forty-rod, sneaking a few swallows, and Rena volunteered a linen undersleeve as a bandage. After dipping his face in the pool, Fargo felt a little woozy but not too sick to head for Dante's View.

40

"Good work, Scotty," Fargo praised.

"Hell, you've saved me and Rena twice," the prospector said. "I still owe you one."

Instead of returning south into the flat trough of Death Valley, they rode up out of Grapevine Canyon and looped around to the slightly less punishing desert bordering the east side of the valley.

Rena gigged her horse up beside the Ovaro. "How long will it take us to ride up there?"

"Couple hours, I guess," Fargo replied, noticing the suppressed excitement in her eyes. "But we're *not* going anywhere else except to the top of the pinnacle."

Rena lowered her voice. "You weren't so stern last night when you came to see me."

"Was Scotty?" Fargo replied from a deadpan.

She reached out to slap his arm. "He said you sent him."

They all mumbled rather than talked, for keeping the mouth closed as much as possible slowed evaporation. The three of them tried to eat in the saddle, jerky and corn dodgers left over from breakfast. However, they were forced to give up—their mouths were too dry to swallow, and there was no future guarantee of water in Grapevine Canyon with the Barton gang around.

"Skye?" Rena said. "While you're watching the valley from Dante's View, may Scotty and I ride over to the bottleneck formation?"

"I already said no. I don't like the idea," Fargo said bluntly.

Her pretty face firmed in defiance under her gaily beribboned straw hat. "Why not? Scotty's sober now. He was able to save me from Barton's gang after they murdered the Pinkerton men."

"First time you've even mentioned them," Fargo said sarcastically. "I guess you were too broke up over it."

"My *point*," she fumed, chin jutting in defiance, "is that I'd be safe with Scotty."

"Say, who'm I?" Scotty cut in. "The redheaded stepchild? Ask *me* if I'm goin', not Skye."

"The problem isn't Scotty," Fargo told her. "It's your damned lies."

"My lies? Balderdash!"

"You don't give a hoot in hell about sketching this area."

41

Fargo pressed the attack. "I looked in your panniers last night—no sketches of this area or anyplace else."

"Looked in my—?" Blood suffused her face. "How dare you—"

"Save it for your memoirs. Whatever you're up to, it has to involve money or valuables, and I'm guessin' they once belonged to someone with the Death Valley Party."

For a moment she was on the verge of more denials. Suddenly her eyes turned shrewd. "That's nonsense, but what if it wasn't? Would that be so bad?"

"Maybe not. But you asked me to do two things: protect you and get you safely to Mission San Fernando so you can take a coach to Boston. That's all I'm doing."

Rena looked ready to throw a tantrum in the saddle. "Who are you, God of the West? It's up to Scotty to decide if—"

"Ain't none of my picnic," the prospector cut in.

"Rena, whack the cork," Fargo snapped, his tone brooking no defiance. "I don't risk my life for treasure hunting, and I sure's hell don't put profit above tracking down woman killers. If you want to look for gold or whatever, get somebody else to help you."

Fargo's long-distance ambush on the Barton gang had caught them completely by surprise. Unable to spot him in the eye-searing glare, and fearful of losing more horses, Mad Dog led the retreat back to the well-hidden abandoned mine known as Busted Flat.

"Boys," Barton said as he swung down off his reddish-gold California sorrel, "that damned Trailsman is startin' to chap my ass, know that? Unless we kill that meddlin' bastard, we're just barkin' at a knot."

"You're the Aunt Nancy who sounded retreat," Taffy Thomas reminded him. "You let one man turn back four, and now you're all horns and rattles over it."

Mad Dog's lips eased back off his long, sharp teeth. Angry yellow eyes like molten metal took Taffy's measure. "Your tongue swings way too loose, whip dick."

Taffy bridled. According to saloon lore, he and Mad Dog were among the fast draw-shoot killers in California and the Southwest. Taffy was in a mood to find out which one was top gunny.

"All right, mouthpiece," the Welshman said, coiling for

the draw. "Jerk one of those shooters and let's get smokin'."

Mad Dog sneered. "Wild and woolly and hard to curry, huh? Boy, you're standing on your own grave."

"*Que necios!*" Pepe Lopez intervened. "What fools! Fargo, this son of a whore, wounds the Kid in his arm and now kills my mare. And *por eso*, for this, you are ready to kill each the other? Father Christ!"

Lopez was a solitary man with cold manners who seldom spoke to his comrades in crime. His heavy-lidded gaze was listless but also deceptive: He was always tensed for action, and his eyes missed nothing.

"The hell you care what we do?" Mad Dog demanded. "No skin off your ass."

Lopez was adjusting the stirrups of a high-cantled saddle for his short legs. With his mare dead, he would be riding a big claybank stallion, one of the two horses stolen when they killed the woman's guards.

"They always talk who never think," he told his leader. "One of you two will die today in this pissing fight. But three of us will still be alive, *verdad?* With one less chance to kill this gringo *cabrón* Fargo. If he is not killed the pretty *artista* will show the entire world our faces. The faces of woman killers. Kill each other *after* Fargo and the others are dead, not before."

Pepe rarely spoke, so when he did the others listened.

"The chilipep is right," Taffy said, sitting down on a pile of ore tailings. "We can't even leave this damn valley until all three are killed."

Mad Dog nodded. "Not 'less we're willing to live in Mexico until we die."

Lopez shook his head. "Not Mexico, *jefe*. Down there we kill a gringo for his boots." He grinned and touched his flattop sombrero with the rattlesnake band. "Or his hat."

Rapid, hollow hoofbeats sounded outside the mine, and all three men filled their hands.

"It's me!" shouted the voice of Kid Papenhagen, who had been riding roving sentry since the ambush.

Papenhagen hobbled his horse outside and rushed into the sloping shaft. "We've *got* him, boys! All three of 'em. They just headed up the Black Mountains toward Dante's View."

Mad Dog whistled. "That's sweet, all right. He's goin' up there to get a good squint at the valley—wants to find where we're holed up. But if we ride out right now, he'll never see us."

"Damn straight," Papenhagen said, staring from hateful eyes at the dirty bandage on his forearm where Fargo had winged him. "There's only one way up and one way down. We can lay for 'em in the scree at the base of the mountains, pay Fargo back for his ambush earlier."

Lopez donned his cross-chest bandolier. Mad Dog's right fist beat the palm of his left hand to underscore his point. "*This* is our best chance, boys, and we can't muck it up. We got the firepower and we'll have surprise on our side. Let's tie a ribbon on this before the word gets out about the Conways."

For almost two hours, as the cruel sun arced higher over Death Valley, Fargo led the way up into the barren Black Mountains. Although steep in places, the riding was fairly easy thanks to solid footing and excellent visibility. Through vast experience in mountain terrain, Fargo led them safely around the few unstable landslide slopes that could send a horse and rider tumbling to their death.

Scotty had the easiest time on General Washington, for mules were more sure-footed than horses. At times the howling wind, always fierce around Death Valley, forced them to grab their hats and blasted them with grit and sand. Dry air sapped the moisture out of them and left all three sucking on bullets to conserve drinking water.

"Skye," Scotty called above the shrieking of wind, "is it true somebody opened a desert way station just north of the valley?"

"I've heard that, too," Fargo replied. "Just above the head of Grapevine Canyon. Never seen it, though."

Rena ignored them, intrigued by the bottleneck-shaped spire of sandstone just off to their left on the next slope. Fargo saw an intense longing in her eyes.

"We can delay a few minutes," Fargo told her, "if you'd like to sketch it real quick. That is, if you can find your sketch pad under all the treasure maps."

Scotty guffawed and Rena raised her chin in defiance.

"No thank you," she replied, her voice revealing hurt dignity. "I'll sketch when we reach the top."

The only signs that men had ever been up these desolate slopes were a few test shafts, abandoned when miners failed to find color. Some silver and gold had been discovered, however, at the edges of the valley below by lone prospectors like Scotty.

Finally the slope leveled off atop the narrow pinnacle called Dante's View. The trio hobbled their mounts and walked forward to the very edge.

"Sakes alive! Not even a blade of grass," Rena marveled. "From here the bed looks like dead ash."

Fighting the fierce wind, she unfolded her canvas stool and began sketching. Straight below them, a mile distant, was a salt-covered pond called Badwater.

"When I see it all at once," Scotty opined, "it makes me feel puny. I never seen so much big empty."

Fargo spent much of his time trying to avoid the net of civilization, which was being cast everywhere. But he had no use for this inhospitable stretch of hell turned inside out. Even Sonora, another pitiless desert, at least had *zopilote*, the great buzzard. Death Valley scared off even carrion birds.

"There's 'life' down there right now," Fargo reminded the prospector. "Two-legged reptiles who slaughter innocent families in their own homes. With a little luck, we'll spot them."

Fargo had already pulled his army field glasses from a saddlebag. Slowly, methodically, he traversed the valley below from east to west and north to south.

"See anything that moves?" Scotty asked.

"Not yet. But both times when the gang ducked our bullets they rode west. I've got a gut hunch they're holed up across the valley from our shack."

"If they was *right* below us," Scotty said, "we couldn't see them."

Fargo nodded. "We've hitched our thoughts to the same tie rail. They could've spotted us riding up and got themselves into ambush position before we got here."

"Our goose is cooked to a cinder if they did."

"Scotty, you're a top hand with rattlesnake bites," Fargo

told him, "but you're a calamity howler. We've got the high ground. I hope they are waiting for us."

The brilliant white glare forced Fargo to avert his eyes. He glanced at Rena's impressive sketch. "Nice work."

"My lands, praise from Caesar," she replied, still miffed about being denied a visit to the bottleneck formation.

Scotty eyed Fargo's saddlebag. "Just a nip, Skye?"

"After dark," the Trailsman said, resuming his search. "You drink liquor in this desert sun, you'll get crazy drunk."

"He gets that way after dark, too," Rena tossed in.

"Ahh, teach your grandmother to suck eggs," Scotty grumped. "Both of you."

For most of the afternoon Fargo patiently searched, but except for whirling dervishes of rock salt and sand he spotted nothing or no one moving. When their shadows were long and thin in the westering sun, he finally lowered the glasses.

"We best head down," he announced to his bored companions.

"This was a waste of time," Rena complained.

"What about your sketch capturing 'artistic and spiritual' Death Valley?" Fargo roweled her. "You know—for your father's magazine."

"Of course," she amended hastily. "Besides that, I meant. We still don't know where the killers are."

"Oh, but I think we do," Fargo gainsaid as he stepped up into leather. "These boys obviously like to ride around plenty. The fact that I didn't spot them once in all this time tells me Scotty just might be right—they're right below us."

Rena's features tightened in sudden fear. "Then why do you appear to be smiling about it?"

Fargo shrugged. "Why do eagles eat lambs?"

Rena looked confused. "But how will we get past them? You yourself said there's only one trail up and down."

"Never mind that for now. You and Scotty need to talk less and pay close attention. If you don't, we'll all be adding lead to our diet."

Fargo led the way, winding down from Dante's View through piles of scree and talus. Their mounts' iron-shod hooves rang loudly on the stone trail. Knowing that was dangerous, Fargo halted them about a thousand feet from the desert floor.

"If they are waiting for us," he said, swinging down, "they'll have to be at the very bottom—this trail's too narrow. No sense announcing our arrival."

Fargo removed a shoeing hammer from a saddlebag and quickly pulled the shoes from the horses and Scotty's mule. He swung up onto the hurricane deck again and slid his Henry from its saddle boot.

"No talk," he warned his charges. "Rena, you ride between me and Scotty."

Fear was starched deep into her features as they resumed the downward trek. With the iron shoes removed, the constant wind noise covered their sounds.

Another five hundred or so feet they rode, and Fargo moved the Henry's hammer from half to full cock. He shucked out his Colt and snapped the wheel out, giving it a quick puff to dislodge any blow sand.

Lower still they wound, Fargo's every sense alert. Mostly, however, he relied on the best sentries he'd ever known—the Ovaro's sensitive ears. The moment he saw them prick forward, Fargo halted his companions.

"Scotty," he whispered, throwing the reins forward to hold the Ovaro in place and lighting down, "you're in charge of Rena now. Watch me, and when I give you the high sign both of you ride like hell. When you get down on the desert floor, *don't* wait for me. Get back into Grapevine Canyon and light a shuck for our new hideout. I'll catch up."

Rocks and boulders crowded both sides of the trail. Fargo picked the left side and began clambering over them, seeking a position where he could see what lay below. Some of the black volcanic rock had knife-sharp edges that sliced into his hands, but the travail was worth it: He eased over a rocky spine and spotted four men well hidden below, weapons at the ready.

The only one he recognized was John "Mad Dog" Barton, a scattergun balanced across the boulder in front of him. Their horses were hobbled well behind them.

Fargo needed a distraction to cover the escape of Rena and Scotty, and it was nestled all around him in the form of boulders. He selected one he hoped he could budge and put his strong back to it, straining. This was a tricky piece of work—if the slide went too far to the right the escape trail would be blocked. So he had to avoid the gang and try to cut them off from their mounts.

His muscles strained like taut cables, the stubborn boulder rocked, then plunged down the steep slope. Each yard it plummeted added more, and within mere moments a bouncing, crashing roar filled the air.

Fargo took off his hat and waved it, sending Scotty and Rena into motion. All four men had covered down to avoid the tumbling boulders, but Fargo had succeeded in missing the trail, and he knew the killers would quickly recover their courage. Now it was up to the Henry, the weapon "you load on Sunday and fire all week," to buy the critical time needed.

Fargo opened up with a vengeance, shooting to kill. He worked the lever rapidly, spraying their position with lead that whined from boulder to boulder. B. Tyler Henry's excellent ejector mechanism clicked flawlessly, and hot brass shell casings rattled against the rocks.

Return fire hammered Fargo's position. A man with a spade beard popped up and drew a bead on him. The Trailsman beat him to the trigger, and the owlhoot's face disappeared in a red smear, his body folding like an empty sack. That unnerved the other three just as Scotty and Rena broke out onto the flat below.

Now Fargo had to get past them before they fully recovered their nerve. He made it back to the Ovaro, vaulted into the saddle, and thumped the stallion's ribs. "Hi-ya! Hii-*ya!*"

The game pinto flew down the trail as Fargo skinned back his single-action Colt and thumb-cocked it. Mad Dog's scattergun worried him most because the killer would be within yards of him, and "aiming" wasn't an issue at close range with a shotgun.

The moment Fargo spotted blued steel he opened up, spacing all six shots. He managed to force Mad Dog's head down, but the other two survivors opened up. Fargo felt the wind rip of several bullets and feared he had pared the cheese too close to the rind. However, heart thumping, he reached the desert floor.

They could not shoot him from their position, nor reach their horses without a hard climb over the rockslide. Fargo reined in. Like most frontier warriors, he figured it was simply manly honesty to derive pleasure from humbling an enemy—making him realize he'd been beaten by a better man.

"Hey, Mad Dog!" he roared out. "One down and three to go! It's fun playin' with girls!"

"You picked the wrong place to come swingin' your eggs, Fargo! Just *try* to get out of this valley!"

"I'm going nowhere, woman killer, until I show your soles to the world."

"You're just whistlin' past the graveyard, Trailsman."

"Good choice of words. This whole area's a graveyard, and I'm planting all three of you in it."

A chorus of filthy curses broke out behind him as Fargo, grinning wickedly, spurred his Ovaro toward Grapevine Canyon.

7

Day bled into night, and a moon bright enough to throw shadows turned Death Valley an eerie, luminous blue. Fargo reached the shack, tucked behind a fantastic jumble of screening boulders, without being followed.

Scotty and Rena had arrived only a few minutes before him, and both were still behind the shack caring for their mounts.

"That was a humdinger of a gun battle, Skye," Scotty said in greeting. "Christ, I like to died when that rock-slide started."

"You could have," Fargo admitted. "It was a roll of the dice."

Scotty said, "The one you sent to eternity is the same sidewinder who cooked my beard. He wasn't inside the Conway cabin when the family was wiped out, so it must be the one the gang called Kid."

Fargo swung down in the grainy twilight and put the Ovaro on a ground tether. "To me, they all got one name: murderers. There's no law out here, so when it comes to justice that's all we got—just us. Don't matter to me if it takes a year. There's three more yellow curs to send under."

"But, Skye," Rena interposed, busy rubbing down her chestnut with a feed sack, "you've wounded one of these men and killed another. What's to stop them from just giving it up as a bad job and leaving Death Valley?"

Fargo pulled his saddle and pad, spreading the wet blanket on a boulder to dry.

"They can't," he replied. "California is a state now, and witnesses saw them rub out the Conway family. Warrants will go out. Matt was a lawman, and lawmen stick together. Even if they dust their hocks all the way to New York, they'll spend the rest of their miserable lives looking over their shoulders. No, they have to kill us right here in the valley and they know it."

Fargo quickly rubbed down his stallion, gave him several hatfuls of tepid water, and strapped a nose bag of oats on him.

"We gonna spell off on guard tonight?" Scotty asked.

"Nah. This shack may be knocked together," Fargo replied, "but at least it's well protected, and the gang can't know we're here—not yet. Besides, my pinto is outlaw savvy, and he'll whinny at the first scent of intruders."

They moved inside, grateful that sundown signaled a rapid cooling of the desert air. Fargo inventoried their remaining food in the meager light of a tallow candle.

"It's running low," he announced. "As of tonight we're all on short rations."

"Hell's bells!" Scotty exclaimed. "They get any shorter, we'll be eatin' air pudding!"

"You won't starve," Fargo promised. "There's food to be had at the upper end of the valley and in Grapevine Canyon."

"Hell, I don't so much mind the bullet in my leg," Scotty grumped. "But Christomighty! At least back in Virginia City a man can keep his beard and eat hot grub. Bean soup and corn bread—that's all I crave."

Rena sat on one of the web bunks, twisting her strawberry blond hair into two thick plaits. "You seem to require more than food once you get drunk," she reminded him.

"And you was buck nekked when I came to your bedroll," Scotty shot back. "What kind of refined Boston lady sleeps in the buff?"

She gave him a quelling stare. "What would you know about ladies? You buy 'love' for a pinch of gold dust."

"Both of you bottle it," Fargo snapped. "Rena, Scotty saved your life, and he might have saved mine when he treated my snakebite. And, Scotty, you launder your talk around a female."

"Ahh, whoopie doodle! *This* female's always got her nose out of joint."

Rena said nothing to this, sending Scotty to hell with her

stare. But when she looked at Fargo, a coquettish smile ousted her frown.

"We'll have to ascend to Dante's View again, won't we?" she asked sweetly.

"I can see you'd like that," he replied. "Just level with me—what the hell are you *really* after?"

"Why, just sketches," she replied, a teasing lilt in her voice.

Scotty bristled like a feist and pulled the rough strip of jerky out of his mouth. "She's a comely lass, all right, Skye. But somethin' 'bout that gal stinks to high heaven. We ain't careful, she'll get us planted."

"Another park bench sage," Rena retorted. "You were more likable when you were drunk all the time, you old reprobate. But at least now perhaps you won't try to climb into my bed."

"Hey, what if I do? The wool of a black sheep is just as warm," Scotty assured her.

In the bat of an eyelash Rena's .41 caliber derringer was aimed at Scotty. "The first time I forgave you. The next time I'll shoot you."

Fargo could have sworn her "Boston Brahmin" accent had weakened. And she was mighty quick with a gun for a lady of the upper crust.

"Hear that, Skye?" Scotty protested.

"You're the one better hear it," Fargo said. "No judge in the land would prosecute her."

"Will we, Skye?" Rena pressed. "Ride up to Dante's View again, I mean?"

"Nix on that," Fargo said, his tone regretful. "They'll be watching for us now. I'll have to track them down from ground level."

Rena looked disappointed but said nothing. Fargo swung open the hide door and went outside to check on their mounts. He rounded the boulder screen and for some time remained out on the flat valley floor, watching millions of stars glitter in the indigo sky. The only sound was the mournful howling of the wind, racing up through the long trough of Death Valley. He pulled his hat low against the stinging grit.

This land was ancient and mysterious, he told himself, like most of the American West. There were still canyons in the Utah Territory that white men had yet to gaze upon, rivers in the Yellowstone country they had yet to navigate. But the miners and lumbermen, the railroad plutocrats and "New York Land Hunters," would eventually despoil all of it. Just as foul murderers were now contaminating the rugged purity of this stark but magnificent valley.

When he went inside, Rena had ducked behind an old calico curtain stretched across a lariat to afford her some privacy. Scotty kicked a three-legged stool out for him.

"Care to test your pasteboard abilities in a friendly game of chance?" the prospector asked him, shuffling a deck of greasy playing cards.

"Sure, but not for money."

"Not even joker poker, penny-ante?"

"Nope," Fargo replied, straddling the stool. "I never plank my cash unless it's a brand-new deck."

Scotty was about to complain, but he caught sight of the liquor bottle Fargo had retrieved from a saddlebag. "Say! That's medicine."

Fargo poured each of them one jolt into a tin cup. Scotty licked his lips to get the last of it.

"Skye," he said as he dealt a hand of stud, "where you think them vermin are holed up?"

"I'd bet my horse it's the west wall of the valley," Fargo replied. "In the shadow of the Panamint Mountains. But that wall's just like this side. There's so many piles of scree and jumbles of boulders it'd take a man a week just to search a mile of it."

"Why search?" Rena's musical voice said from behind her privacy screen. "Dante's View will reveal them. And I could sketch the bottleneck formation."

Scotty sat with his back to her. Rena slid enough curtain aside to let Fargo see her. A chemise of paper-thin muslin showed the plum-colored circles of her nipples. Fargo felt his groin glow warm.

"Still ain't gonna happen," Fargo assured her. "But keep trying to bribe me."

"Oh yes, it *is* going to happen," she assured him right back, yanking the curtain closed again.

Fargo reluctantly slept with his weapons instead of with Rena, his ears attuned to danger. However, the night was still and uneventful except for the soughing of wind in the rocks. He had cooked pan bread the night before so the smoke couldn't be spotted, using one of the crossed-stick shelves for cooking fuel. The three ate a simple breakfast as the sun broke over the Funeral Mountains towering just above them.

"Get horsed," Fargo told both of his companions after breakfast. "We're going to have to ride into Grapevine Canyon so the mounts can tank up good. They'll keel over in this heat if we keep watering them a few swallows at a time."

"Mad Dog's gang already caught us going there once," Rena said fretfully as she followed Fargo behind the shack.

"Put it this way," Fargo replied. "We can run the risk of meeting them again, or we can watch our horses die. Which one sounds smartest to you?"

"Ask her if she wants to leave Death Valley right now," Scotty inserted slyly. "Fir a woman that's s'posed to be scairt of Barton and his cutthroats, she sure seems hell-bent on sticking. *Sketches*, my ampersand."

"Go to blazes!" she snapped, and Fargo had to bite his lip to stifle a laugh. Prospector Scotty had struck a lode.

Luck was with them at this early hour. Nothing moved on the desolate, ash gray landscape. The flat-out emptiness staggered Fargo. The barrel cactus, the organ pipe, the prickly pear, the yucca, the ocotillo, the Joshua tree—none of the common California desert growth existed in Death Valley, where it might be as long as three years between rainfalls.

"You two ride in first," Fargo told them when they reached the wide mouth of the canyon. "Swing well east of the Conway cabin. I'll stand watch out here. When you're finished, you'll wait here while I ride in. Let 'em drink plenty, but stop before they get too logy to run."

When they returned, Fargo kneed his stallion up the rock-littered slope to the upper plateau, well above the valley floor, where Furnace Creek formed its modest but reliable pool. He slipped the bit and loosened the cinch, letting his grateful Ovaro drink deeply. Because horses urinated in the same water they drank, Fargo moved upstream of the pool to fill his canteens and gutbag.

"Spot any trouble?" he asked when he joined the other two.

"Empty as a cowboy's pockets," Scotty replied.

"Maybe they did leave," Rena suggested.

"Won't happen," Fargo insisted, leading them down into the valley again. "Mad Dog got revenge for his brother, but this is one crime they can't ride away from, and they know it. Matter fact, it's a rare woman killer out West who even makes it to court—they have 'accidents' that save the cost of a trial."

They made it back to the shack without spotting the gang, although Fargo couldn't be sure they weren't being observed by someone in hiding—all the more reason why he needed to locate the gang's camp.

"Look, you two," he said, remaining in the saddle after they'd swung down, "it makes no sense for all three of us to ride across the valley, especially since we've got a secure spot here. Scotty, can I count on you to protect Rena while I'm gone?"

Rena surprised Fargo by speaking first. "Of course you can, Skye. He saved me day before yesterday, didn't he, by scaring the gang away?"

Fargo's eyes narrowed in suspicion. "You two been on the scrap with each other lately. All of a sudden you're taking his part?"

"Of course. The fact that he's an old lecher doesn't mean he can't protect me."

Scotty puffed out his chest. " 'At's right. I'm fair to middlin' with a six-shooter, and I know something of the fistic arts, too. And there's always this."

Scotty opened a pannier and brandished the oak war club. "I'll waltz it to 'em with this little honey."

"Uh-hunh," Fargo said, still watching Rena from suspicious eyes. "Just make sure you keep an eye on her, Scotty. Neither one of you goes beyond the screening rocks, understand? If they spot you, Death Valley will be your graveyard."

"Good lands!" Rena scoffed. "Where would we go?"

"I know where you might go," Fargo replied just before he reined the Ovaro around. "And if you do, you're a bigger fool than God made you."

At its upper, or northern, end Death Valley was narrower than at its heart. Fargo reached the west wall of mountains by midmorning, not once pushing the Ovaro past a trot. With two hours left before noon, the summer heat had already turned Fargo's saddle so hot it was hard to sit in. Nor could he produce enough saliva to spit—and if he could have, it would have evaporated before reaching the ground.

Fargo's reputation as a man who could track an ant across granite was severely tested. Much of the valley floor was solid bedrock, and the thin, gray-white powder covering it in places shifted each time the hot wind gusted, which was often. Even so, he was able to find occasional nicks and scratches in the rock, made by iron horseshoes.

Other discoveries were more gruesome, among them a bleached human skeleton, still bent in a crawling position, as he had died while trying to find water. Fargo also spotted a detached human skull, the top caved in—perhaps by the same Indian war club Scotty had found.

Common sense told Fargo the Barton gang could not be holed up too far from Grapevine Canyon—they were obviously using it as a source of water. So he began a thorough search, weaving in and out of the countless clusters of boulders, piles of slag and scree and black volcanic rock that had fallen down the steep slopes of the mountains.

Time dragged by and Fargo's sitter was starting to fry in the inferno his saddle had become. He had just checked yet another potential hiding place and broken out into the open valley again when his heart suddenly turned over: Coming straight at him, perhaps a hundred yards to the south, were three riders.

"Put at the son of a bitch, boys!" bellowed John "Mad Dog" Barton, and the chase was on.

Fargo had great faith in his well-maintained Henry, but it was in its boot and the trio had already opened fire. Rifle and revolver bullets rained in on him, turning the brittle air deadly and humming past his ears with a sound like hornets. Caught flat-footed, and realizing this was a time for discretion over valor, Fargo resorted to the best weapon he possessed: his stallion.

He reined the Ovaro to the north and Grapevine Canyon, not even bothering to thump his horse with his heels. The bullet-savvy pinto broke into a three-beat gallop on its own.

"You're worm fodder now, Trailsman!" Mad Dog bellowed above the hammering racket of gunshots.

At first, before the Ovaro could open out a good lead, Fargo feared the murderer was right. One round punched through the crown of his hat, so close to his skull that it parted his hair. Another *flumped* into the bedroll under his cantle straps.

Fargo knocked the riding thong off the hammer of his Colt, skinned back the weapon, and torqued halfway around in the saddle. The distance was long for a handgun, and aiming was a useless gesture when bouncing along at a heady gallop. But he drilled six fast shots into the pursuers, close enough to let some of the steam out of their pursuit.

Still, however, the lead kept pouring in, and Fargo knew they were trying for the biggest target—his horse. His only chance to shake them was to reach Grapevine Canyon and its maze of boulders. But the stalwart Ovaro, who had already endured this hellish heat for hours, was beginning to lather hard. Could he make it without collapsing?

Fargo bent low over the stallion's neck. "C'mon, old warhorse," he urged. "It's up to you now, boy. Just get us to the canyon, and I'll take over."

Man and horse raced on, death snapping at their heels.

8

"You know, Scotty," Rena said coyly soon after Fargo rode out, "Skye is a brave and good man. But he *is* awfully strict, don't you think?"

Both of them were seated at the trestle table, where Rena was rendering the prospector's likeness in charcoal.

Scotty pulled at his ruined whiskers, watching her from cautious eyes. "Strict? Why, not so's you'd notice. It's just we need to stay disciplined is all. We got killers tryin' to blow out our lamps, and the worstest desert in the world all around us."

She nodded, shading in his eyebrows. "Of course. I'm not being catty. But I don't see any good reason why you can't enjoy a drink now and then."

He sighed tragically. "*That* shines. What I'd give right now to be a fish in an ocean of whiskey."

"So who's stopping you?"

The prospector snorted. "Are you forgettin' he poured all my liquor out 'cept that one bottle? And he's got the dad-blamed thing in his saddlebags."

"He *had* the bottle," she said, correcting him. "I have it now."

Scotty goggled at her. "You got it?"

Her pretty face was divided by a smile of complicity. "Yes. While Skye was cooking last night I put the bottle in my art-supplies bag. I have it right here."

Joy sparked in the old-timer's eyes, followed almost immediately by grave suspicion. "Why would you do that fir an 'old lecher' like me?"

"Don't be silly! I called you that because I was in a foul mood. I like mature men."

58

"You do?"

"I should say so. Have you heard the saying 'The older the violin the sweeter the music'?"

Scotty squirmed as he took her meaning. "You smacked *this* old violin hard enough to break his strings when I came a-visitin' the other night."

"Land sakes, Scotty, you don't just attack a woman in her bed! We like to be sweet-talked a little."

"I reckon that's so. But I'd need a little oil of gladness to sweeten my tongue."

Rena reached into her bag and set the bottle in front of him. "Sweeten away."

He reached for it, but then pulled his gnarled hand back. "I dunno. Skye ain't gonna like this."

"You didn't filch it. I did. Besides, he won't miss a little more of it—nobody misses a slice off a cut loaf."

"Truer words and all that." Scotty pulled the cork with his teeth and knocked back a slug, smacking his lips. "Yessir, that's medicine."

He stared at the topaz contents of the bottle, torn between his love of drink and his sense of duty.

"That swallow didn't seem to bring the level down at all," Rena remarked, still sketching.

"Didn't, did it?" Scotty agreed. "I hate to hedge when it comes to good whiskey."

He tipped the bottle again, failing to notice the satisfied smile on Rena's full red lips.

The Ovaro performed heroically in the punishing climate, even surpassing a gallop and breaking into a headlong run for the last mile or so to the mouth of the canyon. The gang had dropped at least a quarter mile behind Fargo by that time, giving him just enough time to enter the canyon, slip into a dry wash, and ride behind a wall of giant boulders, some larger than houses.

He had no intention of simply hiding while his enemies searched for him. Three-to-one odds were not daunting to Fargo, especially when he held a good position. They expected him to hole up like a rabbit, but the Trailsman always preferred the offensive—it took the fighting confidence out of a foe.

Fargo levered a round into the Henry's chamber. The

moment Mad Dog Barton broke through the mouth of the canyon on his reddish-gold sorrel, Fargo began peppering all three men. Bullets whanged from boulder to boulder, creating high, whining sounds from repeated ricochets.

As Fargo had predicted, they immediately reversed course and escaped onto the valley floor without firing a shot. However, he didn't leave it at that. He'd deliberately picked a spot where he could quickly scramble to a higher position and toss more lead at them while they fled. The redhead cried out, blood spuming from a hit to his right calf, and that tore it for the attack. The trio raised dust back toward the west wall of the valley.

Fargo thumbed reloads into the Henry's tube magazine and the cylinder of his Colt. Then he scrambled back down to the Ovaro and rode farther up the canyon, watering the thirsty stallion from his hat. By now the afternoon heat was at its worst, and the boulders reflected it with merciless intensity. Still, Fargo allowed a little more time before riding out.

He hugged the shadowed east wall as he returned to the shack. He considered his search a partial success. True, he hadn't spotted the precise location where the gang emerged from the screening boulders. But they hadn't ridden out into the open yet the last time he'd ducked in to search the scree, which gave him a good idea where to find them.

Fargo reined in and rode behind the shack. "That sneaky *bitch*," he cursed when he saw that Rena's chestnut was missing. Fargo didn't even consider foul play—not when he recalled the way she'd acted when he left. She was off on her damned treasure hunt.

He found Scotty sprawled on his web bed. The shack stank like a vat of corn mash, and the last liquor bottle sat empty on the table.

"You damned drunken sot," Fargo snarled, hauling the prospector to his feet and shaking him until his teeth clacked like dice. "Wipe that grin off your map, you old fool. Who told you to sneak that bottle from my saddlebag?"

"Don't lay it at my door," Scotty protested. "Rena took it while you was cookin' last night. She got me drunk and snuck off when I fell asleep."

"Never mind the weak excuses. You were s'posed to watch her, knothead. And you did a bang-up job."

"She's the mother of the devil," Scotty muttered. "Dad-gasted female."

Fargo never stayed angry long with a friend. He let go of Scotty and began pacing the shack.

"I know where she went," he mused aloud. "How long ago did she leave?"

"Mebbe two hours ago."

"Hmm . . . there's a chance she climbed up out of sight while I was keeping the gang busy. Problem is, if she rides down while it's still light enough, good odds they'll spot her. She needs to descend after sunset, and I don't trust that lady-broke chestnut of hers on a dark trail."

Fargo lived by quick, decisive plans, and he made one now. "Scotty, my stallion is done in. Your mule looks like a sturdy mount, and he made it up and down that trail to Dante's View without slipping once. Would he accept me in the saddle?"

"Sure. He knows your scent. General Washington ain't a temperamental animule. Take him, Skye, and if he sulls on you, just tickle his ribs. Puts 'm in a good mood."

"One more thing," Fargo said as he grabbed Scotty's saddle and bridle and swung open the hide door. "Wouldja mind rubbing down my horse and running a currycomb over him? You'll have to strip the tack, too."

"Least I can do," Scotty admitted, "after gumming up the works like I done."

"The least," Fargo agreed.

As he stepped outside into the heat and glare, Scotty called out, "Be careful, Skye. I don't trust Rena any more than I do the Barton gang. I'm a drunken fool, mebbe, but *that* gal is six sorts of bad trouble."

Fargo knew, as he rode Scotty's mule up the face of the Black Mountains, that he might be spotted himself. Even so, it was better than running the risk of letting Mad Dog's bunch catch Rena coming down alone.

General Washington was a good-natured mule and gave the Trailsman little trouble beyond a rough gait. He negoti-ated loose shale slopes and steep facets with sure-footed ease.

The westering sun burned with weight on Fargo's back, and the desert wind howled like souls in hell, grit stinging him with the force of buckshot. Just before the trail made its final, corkscrew twist to the pinnacle called Dante's View, Fargo reined off onto a natural saddle. It led across to the massive sandstone formation that had been carved, by aeons of harsh, blasting wind, into the bottleneck formation that so intrigued Rena.

"Here's trouble," Fargo muttered when he saw, just ahead, Rena's riderless chestnut, still saddled. The gelding seemed on the verge of panic, but Fargo soothed it with patient talk until he could finally seize the bridle reins.

About fifty yards farther he spotted Rena lying motionless on the hard stone surface, her crushed straw hat beside her. A huge chunk of slag lay nearby, and when Fargo glanced overhead he guessed what had happened: The slag had broken loose from a turret above and spooked her horse.

Expecting to find her dead or dying, Fargo swung down and quickly hobbled the mule and the gelding. Rena failed to respond to his voice, and a grape-colored bruise covered her right temple. But her breathing was strong, and she woke instantly when Fargo splashed her face with canteen water.

Her long, curving eyelashes fluttered open. "Skye! Oh, am I dreaming?"

"You little fool," he said without heat. "Has your brain come unhinged? Between you and Scotty, I might's well be hauling kids around. *Sneaky* kids."

Carefully, he helped her sit up. "Anything hurting besides your head?"

"Just the place where I sit, and it's only sore from the hard landing. I didn't hit my head until I rolled. But, sakes and saints! It's so *hot* in this sun!"

Fargo sent a dubious glance around them. "I don't know where to get you out of it."

"Straight ahead, at the base of the formation," she told him, "there should be a cavern entrance."

"Uh-*hunh*," he replied as he helped her up. "A cave? And I noticed your art bag back in the shack. Well, whatever you came up here for, I hope it's worth your life. Mad

Dog Barton and his skunk-bit toadies could have the trail down blocked by now. C'mon."

The huge sandstone formation was just ahead of them, so he untied the hobbles and led both animals, supporting Rena with his free arm.

"There!" she called out above the racket of wind, pointing to an erosion cave in the face of the sandstone.

Fargo led their mounts inside and hobbled them again near the entrance, where the light was generous. The thick stone walls made it blessedly cooler. Rena's initial excitement began to fade when a quick examination revealed a vast cavern of interconnecting chambers, some as small as a stagecoach, others as big as Mrs. Astor's ballroom.

"Not enough light to explore all of it," Fargo said, leading her back toward the entrance. "Now, how 'bout it? The hell you looking for up here?"

"I told you before—"

"Give," he commanded.

Rena sighed and appeared to surrender. "Jewels," she replied bluntly. "Jewels valued at almost one hundred thousand dollars."

Fargo looked skeptical. "Have you been listening to pub lore back east? We may be the first white people who ever stepped foot in here."

"Not the first," she insisted. "Didn't I tell you that my newlywed sister and her husband were among the Death Valley Party of 1849?"

"You said that, yeah."

"When Sarah and her husband, James, left Boston they had a cherrywood box with them, well hidden in their wagon. The jewelry inside was my mother's, family heirlooms handed down for countless generations. By tradition, it went to the oldest daughter upon her marriage."

Fargo nodded. "All that sounds jake. But why would it be up here?"

"With most of the party dead or dying, James rode up to Dante's View hoping to spot water outside the valley— they must not have known about Furnace Creek. He hid the jewels somewhere in this cavern."

Fargo raised skeptical brows. "How would you know that?"

"Before she died, Sarah managed to scrawl a coded message, and the few survivors who finally found Furnace Creek mailed it back to the Commonwealth of Massachusetts. A Pinkerton man sent out by my father was killed by Mohave Indians before he could pinpoint the 'bottleneck' shape my sister mentioned."

Even as she explained all this, Rena moved around the outer cavern, eyes looking everywhere.

"So, with one daughter and a Pinkerton dead," Fargo said, "your father sends *another* daughter to locate those jewels?"

"They shouldn't be too hard to find," Rena mused aloud, neatly sidestepping his question.

"Parts of your story are prob'ly true," Fargo conceded. "But like I said, I'm not here to help you get rich—"

"Rich?" she protested. "But—"

"Put a stopper on your gob," he ordered. "I'm not going to enrich you at the cost of my life, nor am I interested in anything but justice for the Conway family. While I'm responsible for you, you'll do what I say. Come back here on your own time if you're seeking a fortune."

A sudden anger squall rose inside her. "Skye Fargo, I'm talking about family heirlooms!"

"Maybe so, but not *your* family."

"Skye, that's preposterous! How in Mary's grace would I know so much if—"

He waved this off. "Don't know and don't care. No sane man would send his daughter to do what a Pinkerton man died trying to do."

Her nostrils flared. "I had *two* Pinkertons with me, don't forget."

"Doesn't mean your father hired them."

A long silence filled the cavern except for the shrieking howl of the wind outside.

"All right." She finally surrendered. "Father is an old sobersides, Skye. I admit I came out without his permission. But I have a right to be here."

A wry smile tilted one corner of Fargo's mouth. "Just curious—have you visited your sister's grave? You must know where it is since there were survivors."

"I—that is—I'm going to," she faltered out, Fargo enjoying a strong laugh at her obvious deceptions.

"I'm gonna read the book to you, girl, and you'd best listen," he told her. "To me, these jewels you obviously lust after are nothing but a bunch of damned flubdubs. We're waiting up here until after dark, and then we're heading down. Period. We're *not* coming back up here."

Rena was still searching, but the cavern was huge, and the rest of the chambers would require plenty of time—and more light—to search properly.

"Dash!" she exclaimed, stamping her foot in frustration. "I'll never find anything this way."

Her moods were mercurial. She slanted a sly glance at Fargo. Her fluid, impulsive lips eased into a seductive smile, and she walked toward the mule and the gelding, unstrapping the bedrolls from both cantles. Rena spread them both together to soften the surface.

"Long as we have to wait," she said suggestively, "why don't you stretch out and get comfy?"

Fargo did just that, opening his fly in anticipation. "I notice how you always cozy up to me when you want something."

"So what? Do you mind?"

He watched her shuck out of her split riding skirt and long shirtwaist, and unbutton her ankle shoes before peeling off her ruffled pantaloons. She stood above him, both firm ivory tits capped by huge nipples like luscious plums. Her strawberry-tinted blond hair now cascaded over her shoulders.

"Mind?" he repeated, guiding his throbbing erection out of his trousers. "Hell no. I'm not sensitive. Besides, your strategy won't work. But get down here and give it your best."

Rena's long, supple legs straddled him and she bent him to the perfect angle, lining the throbbing dome of his manhood up with her dewy lips and plunging down onto him. She moaned with feral pleasure, gyrating her hips and shooting hot jolts of pleasure from his staff to his groin.

"*God*, you fill a girl up," she gasped, moving faster as pleasure greed took hold of her.

Fargo took each of her spearmint-tasting nipples into his mouth in turn, sucking, kissing, biting, until they were stiff and long. Now she cried out in hot abandon, moving up to the very tip, then plunging to the base of his length. To

Fargo, it felt like his entire shaft was sliding into a tight velvet glove, working it into a hot, tickling, pleasurable frenzy.

"There!" she cried out, moving so recklessly Fargo had to balance her with a hand on each butt cheek. "*That's* it! I—I—oh, Skye, I'm ex-*plod*ing!"

An intense climax tore a cry from her as Fargo, too, spent himself inside her, requiring half a dozen powerful thrusts to finish. Exhausted by their passion, both of them slipped into a postclimactic daze. Even as he drifted, however, Fargo reminded himself there was only one way down to the valley floor—and if the Barton gang was waiting in hiding like before, he was fresh out of tricks for saving his and Rena's lives.

9

"You boys are frettin' and steamin' over nothing," Mad Dog Barton scoffed at his two remaining companions. "We came within an ace of killin' Fargo today. Hell, next time we *will*. Only fools would give up now. We can't let him go, and you know it."

Barton, Taffy, and Pepe had returned to their hideout in the Busted Flat mine. Taffy had tied a bandanna around his wounded right calf, but blood was steadily oozing through the cloth.

"Bilge!" the Welshman snapped at his boss. "This Skye Fargo is double rough. He killed Pepe's mare, he shot me, he wounded the Kid, and now he's *killed* the Kid. All that, and we ain't even touched him. We need to haul our freight outta here and cut our losses."

Mad Dog farted with his lips. "Ah, t'hell with the Kid, Taffy. He wouldn't've pissed in your ear if your brains was on fire. 'Sides, he was a coward. Hell, I'da shot him by now 'cept for his skill at crackin' locks and safes."

"He ain't the issue," Taffy hotly insisted. "Fargo is. That jasper is a good man to let alone."

Pepe Lopez spoke up. "*Eso es loco*. We cannot let him alone. If he survives this valley, this means the woman and the *anciano*, the old man, also survive. We will spend the rest of our days with a—how do you say?—posse behind us. We will not even take a crap in peace."

Mad Dog nodded enthusiastically. "Them's the hard-cash facts, Taffy. Think about it. If you've got a sliver in your finger, do you cut your arm off at the elbow?"

"Actually," Taffy reminded him, "me and Pepe got *no*

slivers in our fingers—we never once pulled a trigger. You killed all three of the Conways."

"Sure, on account you were busy playin' stinky finger with the daughter. Don't kid yourself—all three of us will wear hemp neckties."

Taffy loosed a hot string of curses. "Go ahead and talk the he-bear talk. *You* ain't just been shot! Feels like a branding iron on my leg."

"Ah, stop your damn caterwaulin'," Mad Dog scoffed. "Pepe ain't showin' yellow, why should you? You're s'pose to be a shootist. Act like one."

Taffy's florid face turned as red as his hair. "*S'pose* to be a shootist? When a man calls me yellow, that's as good as callin' me out."

Taffy rose from his seat on a pile of ore tailings, coiling for the draw. "You got two fancy guns stickin' out of that sash. Jerk one of 'em."

Pepe, busy running a whetstone over his ten-inch bowie, smoothly intervened.

"*Vaya!* Both of you are *hombres de veras* and pistoleros to be feared. Why kill each the other? Better to kill Fargo, *verdad*?"

This ended the tension. Taffy sat back down, and Mad Dog nodded agreement. "That gets my money, Pepe. This lanky bastard Fargo is known as a frontiersman, not a draw-shoot killer. He don't stand deuce-high against me 'n' you, Taffy."

"I guess that's so," the Welshman conceded. "But look where we caught him today—close to our hideout. Won't be long, he'll find this place."

Mad Dog nodded. "He might, but don't forget, we got a replacement coming—one a helluva lot more useful than that chicken-gutted kid."

Taffy's face brightened. "*Hell* yes—Fenton is due to get out of the calaboose in Los Angeles, ain't he?"

"Might be out already," Mad Dog said. "I left word for him to join up with us. Ain't no man alive can handle a Sharps Big Fifty like him."

"That's fine and dandy *if* he comes," Taffy pointed out. "We can't count on it. Fargo needs to be freed from his soul, and mighty damn quick."

"That's scripture," Mad Dog agreed. "Bastard thinks he

can run one flimflam after another on us. But we'll steal a march on Fargo, find him before he finds us."

"How? This valley is big. Keeping track of one man is like tryin' to find a sliver in an elephant's ass."

Shrewdness seeped into Mad Dog's yellow eyes. "It's a lot smaller if you only search the part that matters. He can't be too far south because they need the water at Furnace Creek. And we'd've spotted him before now if he was on our side of Death Valley."

"He's hiding in the base of the Black Mountains, all right," Taffy agreed. "Or else the Funeral range close by. I still say Pepe should be out there watching the slopes. Hell, Fargo climbed them once."

"Nah, he just rode up to Dante's View to see if he could find us, is all. Ain't likely he'll try that again. That's why he just decided to search the valley on horseback."

Besides the ivory-and-silver revolvers in his fancy embroidered sash, Mad Dog always hauled two loaded scatterguns around with him. He hefted one of the 12-gauge sawed-offs leaning against the side of the mine shaft.

"Revolvers are handy, boys," he told his men. "But the way I see it, most threats are usually close in where a man's got no time to aim. Fargo and them other two are most likely in some abandoned shebang, and *this* little puppy can clear out a room quicker than a spraying skunk. Just stick it into a window at night and squeeze both triggers. Whoever ain't killed by the blast, we'll gun down when they run out."

Mad Dog pointed with the sawed-off toward the mine entrance. A nascent moon, huge and bright white, was balanced atop the dark silhouette of the Funeral Mountains.

"How 'bout it?" he demanded. "We ride out after dark tonight and start searching that east wall."

Taffy and Pepe exchanged a glance. Both men nodded.

"All right," Mad Dog said, his voice pleased. "Nuff goddamn jawboning. The sooner we get it done, the quicker we get out of this frying pan."

Full dark had descended by the time Fargo tied a double half hitch in the lead line connecting Rena's chestnut to the saddle horn of Scotty's mule.

"Hold the reins, but let General Washington take us

down," he instructed Rena as he lifted her effortlessly into the saddle. "The only thing more sure-footed than a mule is a mountain goat."

"It's not the ride down I'm worried about," she confessed. "It's the possible reception committee at the bottom."

"That didn't stop you from sneaking up here, did it?"

"The gamble would have been worth it if I'd found those—I mean, my sister's jewels."

Fargo gave a sarcastic bark as he swung up into leather. "You can lie about as good as Scotty holds liquor."

"Aren't I good at *some* things?" she teased, reminding him of their time in the cavern.

"I can't deny it. Just be damn sure you never come up here again."

"I won't," she said, not making it a promise.

The first part of the journey down to the desert floor from Dante's View in the Black Mountains was uneventful except for treacherous wind that pitted their skin with gravel and sand. About halfway down, Fargo was forced to halt and dismount so he could reset Scotty's saddle—the steep angle of descent had thrown it off center.

"Skye?" Rena said during a lull in the wind.

"Hmm?"

"You mentioned how the gang almost caught you today. Do you still plan to keep looking for their hideout?"

"I think I know where they must be, or at least, priddy near," he replied as he tightened the girth. "But I've lost the element of surprise now. They'll be watching."

"Can we get past them if they're waiting below?"

"We won't likely *slip* past them," Fargo admitted as he stirruped and swung up onto the hurricane deck. "Trail's too narrow. But that doesn't mean we're gone beavers. Just means it'll be a tricky piece of work. Only a fool plans to die."

When they had reached a small shelf before the final, steep descent, Fargo again halted them, this time to let the mule and the chestnut blow in case a hard run lay ahead. Fargo stood up in the stirrups to see better, but detected nothing in the moon-washed boulders below them.

"All right," he whispered to Rena, "hang on like a tick.

We're gonna steam down outta here like the Wabash express running late."

Fargo skinned back his Colt, cocked it, and thumped his boot heels hard into the mule's ribs. By the time they hit the flat plain below, rocks sliding before them, he knew their clover was deep—Mad Dog's gang was nowhere around them.

"Skye, we're safe!" Rena exulted while Fargo untied the lead line.

"We got lucky," he conceded. "But don't forget—last time they tried to ambush us at the base of the mountains, one of 'em got hurled into eternity. We still have to keep our noses to the wind when we ride through Grapevine Canyon. There's plenty of good ambush spots there."

In the canyon they filled their canteens at Furnace Creek before letting the thirsty mounts tank up. As they emerged from the mouth of the canyon onto the hard floor of Death Valley, Fargo reined in and swung down.

"Hold these," he told Rena, handing her his reins and then lying flat on the ground.

"What in the world are you doing?" she demanded.

"It's called skylining. Plains Indians use it a lot."

Skylining would have been worthless toward the east and west, where mountains completely darkened the sky. Straight south, however, was nothing but the long, unbroken trough of Death Valley. For long minutes Fargo peered in that direction.

"See anything?" Rena's impatient voice finally broke in.

"Hard to say," he replied, standing up and brushing the rock salt from his fringed buckskins. "I thought I saw three shapes that might have been horsebackers. But all this swirling grit confused the issue."

"Which way were they riding?"

"From the Panamints on the west toward our side."

Fargo took the reins from her and forked leather. "Damn this place anyway! Almost everything I've ever learned about tracking and scouting is worthless. Well, it's best to assume I did see Mad Dog's gang and that they're trying to sniff us out."

Fargo gigged General Washington forward, sliding his Henry from the saddle boot. They hugged the inky fathoms of shadow at the base of the mountains and reached the hidden shack without incident.

Scotty heard them ride around back and emerged from the shack to greet them. "Well, if it ain't my one true woman," he told Rena sarcastically. "The gal who likes to play *old violins*."

"You fell for it, you old fool, clear through the floor," she retorted as she stripped the leather from her chestnut. "Don't try to shame me."

"You're past shame, you connivin' hussy! I oughter—"

"Bottle it," Fargo snapped. "Both of you. Scotty, knock us up some grub."

"Huh! We're about to run dry on eats. You'll hafta gnaw on salt pork."

Rena made a face at the smelly stuff, but Fargo—who could eat the tar paper off a shack in starving times—chewed a few bites while he quickly rubbed down the mule.

"Mad Dog and his toadies might be on our side of the valley," he told Scotty. "It's a safe bet they're looking for us. You and me'll be on sentry duty tonight, switching off every three hours."

"What, while Her Nibs gets her beauty sleep?" Scotty protested. "She can sneak off into the mountains by her lonesome, can't she? Let her pull equal shares."

"Pipe down," Fargo ordered. "Just remember: Stand watch out in front, not back here. If you see anybody drawing near, don't shoot—wake me up. I'll take the first guard."

Fargo took his rested Ovaro out in front of the screening rocks with him, not to ride but for the added security of those sensitive ears. It was a wise decision: Almost immediately, the pinto's ears pricked toward the south.

"I was right," Fargo muttered. "They're on the prowl."

He couldn't see them yet, but he trusted his horse. Fargo knew it was critically important not to mark this spot with gunfire, or he would have to find a new hideout. With trouble approaching, he quickly hobbled the Ovaro behind the shack, then headed south on foot, sticking to the cover of rocks and scree.

Fargo kept a constant eye on the open valley floor as he walked perhaps a half mile. Abruptly, he heard the clinking rattle of bit rings, the creak of leather. He dropped to his

knees and, peering out through boulders, watched the sil-
houettes of three riders glide by.

He let them trot past, then jacked a round into the Henry's chamber and slipped out from cover to take up a prone
position behind the trio. He cursed his luck—the pale wafer
of ivory moon, as well as an infinity of twinkling stars, was
obscured by a curtain of swirling dust. Had the wind
abated, he might have picked off one or two of the enemy.
Instead, he could see nothing out ahead.

Nonetheless, he knew they were there. Fargo planted his
left elbow, rested the Henry's wooden stock against his
cheek, and opened fire with grim determination.

Again and again the stock slapped his cheek as Fargo
levered and fired, the repeater's muzzle spitting orange
streaks. Knowing Mad Dog's gang could see his muzzle fire,
he rolled to a new spot every few shots, unrelenting in his
attack. Rapidly, he emptied all sixteen rounds in his
magazine.

The gang snapped a few rounds off in his direction, one
lucky shot even kicking rock salt into Fargo's eyes. But
their defense was halfhearted—rattled by the sudden spray
of lead, they reined west and galloped off across the flat
trough of Death Valley like butt-shot dogs.

By instinct, Fargo reloaded before he did anything else.
The attack had gone just as he'd hoped, and they never
got a fix on the location of the shack. Still, it was not the
Trailsman's way to wage defensive battles. As he pushed
to his feet he resolved yet again: These three killers had to
be flushed out of hiding, and soon.

The longer it dragged out, the more likely it was that
Fargo and his companions would be joining the Conways.

10

At sunrise the next morning, the last of Fargo's coffee and Scotty's hardtack wafers furnished their meager breakfast.

"My teeth can't even break it," Rena complained, rapping the hardtack on the trestle table.

"Let it soak in your coffee," Fargo suggested, calmly brushing a weevil off it for her.

"Skye, we figgered you for a gone-up case when that shootin' commenced last night," Scotty said. "Think you plugged any of 'em?"

"Not likely," Fargo replied. "Couldn't even see my targets, and they were in motion. But at least the sound of sixteen slugs buzzing past their ears scared 'em off."

"Way things are lookin'," Scotty said, his scraggly-bearded face grim, "they won't have to air us out with lead. Starvation will either kill us or drive us out of the valley."

Fargo shook his head, remembering the five bodies he buried. "Nix on that. We don't pull foot until Mad Dog and his fellow curs are shoveling coal in hell."

Scotty suddenly squinted suspiciously. "H'ar now! Ain't nobody eatin' my mule. General Wash—"

"Stow it." Fargo cut him off. "We're headed out this morning to stock up on food."

Rena looked horrified. "Not those saltwater sardines you mentioned?"

Fargo grinned wickedly. "Why not? There's a water-course called Salt Creek in the upper valley. Only flows aboveground for about a mile before the sand swallows it up. The sardines are less than an inch long, but nourishing."

"I've et worse grub," Scotty said. "But it's a mighty thin diet, ain't it?"

"We'll have something better," Fargo promised. "At the base of the Panamints there's a few natural wells with vegetation around them, including mesquite trees. Mesquite pods can be smashed into tasty meal. Indians have lived on mesquite bread for centuries."

"Indians!" Rena repeated. "My lands, I've read they eat boiled puppies."

Fargo nodded. "That's easier than frying them."

Rena made a disgusted sound in her throat and ran outside, Fargo and Scotty enjoying a good belly laugh. Moments later, however, Fargo looked deadly serious.

"We're going to be in plain view at both places," he warned Scotty. "And when we harvest those mesquite pods, we'll be close to Mad Dog's bunch. We might have to make a stand in the open. Take all the water you can."

They saddled up and rode out after breakfast, Fargo hoping to avoid the killer heat of the midday sun. He decided to visit the Panamints first, knowing criminals were a lazy breed who slept late. Perhaps his hunch was right—they filled Rena's saddle panniers with plenty of mesquite pods and got under way again with no challenges.

"This desert sun and air are terrible for a girl's skin," she carped as they headed north toward the upper valley.

"There, there," Fargo soothed in a mocking tone. "That's a tough old soldier."

After a moment's angry indignation, she joined the two men in laughing at herself. However, Fargo noticed her gaze kept returning to that bottleneck formation in the mountains. *There'll be more trouble on that score*, he assured himself.

At Salt Creek they found scores of sardines trapped in pockets of muddy water. However, Fargo found something else that took him by surprise—the rumors were true about a way station. He spotted it well beyond them on the rim of the valley, where the southern trail led to the Comstock Lode—a dilapidated structure of raw planks.

"Why, they may have decent food!" Rena exclaimed as Fargo crammed sardines into a saddlebag. "Can't we ride up there, Skye?"

Fargo remained silent, annoyed at the sight of "progress" on the edge of this remote, pristine valley. A man could still ride between El Paso and the Canadian Rockies without seeing one fence, but he'd find mines, banks, and railroad offices—fences wouldn't be far behind.

"Not a good idea," he replied. "I doubt there's any 'decent' food anyway, and a place this remote is likely an outlaw haven."

Rena looked disappointed but nodded. "I take your point. Barton's gang could be up there right now."

"Hmm . . . that's right," Fargo said as he hit the stirrup and pushed up and over. "Might not be such a bad idea after all. Better to face them and get it over with."

"Besides," Scotty tossed in, "they'll have coffin varnish. *Christ*, I'm dried to jerky."

"Just one drink," Fargo warned the prospector as they reined toward the north. "And you can buy one bottle, but it stays with me."

Letting their mounts walk in the scorching heat, the trio made their way up the valley and climbed over the brim on a series of natural staircase ledges. A crudely painted sign over the split-slab door identified the desert way station as the Scorpion's Lair. Fargo studied the half dozen horses tied to a snortin' post in front of the weather-sapped building, but none of them was familiar.

"Looks like our owlhoots aren't here," he said, his tone disappointed. "But this place looks like trouble—those are outlaws' mounts. Look how they're scarred in the shoulders from hard spurring and galled from tight girths. Don't turn your back on this bunch."

They watered their mounts at a trough beside the snortin' post, but chose to hobble them in the shade of the building. Inside, the place reeked of onions, whiskey, sweat, and tobacco. Even painting, plastering, and paper hanging, had there been any, could not have helped the Scorpion's Lair look more inviting. Besides a long plank bar along one wall, the only furnishings were upended packing crates and empty powder kegs.

Rena sniffed the foul and rancid air. "Forget the food," she murmured to Skye. "Smells like it's already been digested."

Fargo, however, kept a wary eye on the hardcases scattered around, drinking. One, especially, looked like sure trouble—a hulking, pox-scarred bully boy playing with a whip made of a five-foot hickory stick and a twelve-foot buckskin lash. Like every other man in the place, he was eyeing Rena with open hunger.

"Name your poison," said a toothless old hag behind the bar.

"Whiskey for me," Scotty ordered, "and slop it over the brim."

Fargo planted his elbows carefully to avoid the beer spatters on the bar. "Beer," he told the crone. "Have you got a Dr. Wyler's for the lady?"

Snickers moved through the barroom at mention of this popular sarsaparilla. "*That* caps the climax," Pox Scars remarked so all could hear.

While the serving woman turned to get their drinks, Scotty muttered, "Looks like she's been rode hard and put up wet one time too many."

"Your lucky day, sugar britches," mouthed off the bully boy, leering at Rena. "I own this place and I don't charge no stud fee. Come have a real drink with me."

The old woman banged down their drinks. "It's two bits apiece for the whiskey and the sugar tonic. The beer'll cost you a short bit."

Fargo shifted his Henry to his left hand and planked his dime.

"Say, darlin'," the proprietor thundered out, "I reckon you're too fine-haired to drink with me, anh?"

Fargo drained his warm, flat beer in one long pull. He sleeved foam off his lip and said in a mild tone, "The lady's with me, mister."

The troublemaker's face twisted with coarse insolence. "Well, if it ain't Joe Shit the Ragman, tryin' to act like he's *some*. If there's one thing I don't hardly need, Davy Crockett, it's a bearded bastard in buckskins tryin' to play Lord Grizzly. Why'n'cha go check your beaver traps while me 'n' the boys drain our snakes in—*Christ!*"

Rena, who Fargo knew had a hair-trigger temper, suddenly spun around and hurled her sarsaparilla at the mouthpiece. It missed his greasy-haired head by inches.

"Go to hell, you filthy, stinking brute!" she also hurled at him.

"Ain't she in a fine pucker?" he asked his audience, suddenly pushing to his feet. "Boys, we can't tell if the wood is good just by lookin' at the paint. Let's strip her buck."

He advanced a few steps before Fargo turned from the bar to face him. "You know, Scotty," he said affably, "when I woke up this morning, I was *sure* I wouldn't have to kill a man today. 'Pears I was wrong."

The bully's jaw went slack with surprise, but he quickly recovered his bluster. " 'Case you ain't noticed, asshole, I'm the big he-dog hereabouts. This here's my groggery."

"That would explain the stink. Now let me give you your only warning you'll get from me: Back off and shut up. You're drunk, which is why I haven't killed you by now. But I'm out of patience."

The bully boy, snapping his whip, looked at the others drinking with him. "Ahh, he's just running a bluff. Let's call in his cards, boys."

Fargo's face closed like a vault door. The lash suddenly hissed toward him, but the Trailsman's lightning-swift left hand caught it. Fargo flipped his Henry to Scotty. "Cover the others. Shoot the first son of a bitch who even twitches."

Fargo's attacker was too stupid to let go of the whip. Fargo reeled him closer with a hard tug, jerking him wildly off balance. He continued pulling until the loudmouth's face cracked hard into the edge of the plank counter, knocking out most of his remaining teeth and savagely pulping his lips.

The man collapsed in howling agony, but Fargo had no intention of letting a potential rapist and killer off that easy. He grabbed each hand in turn and swiftly, methodically bent all the fingers straight back at once until they snapped at the first joint like green wood. The screams of pain, shrill and almost inhuman, made the other customers turn pale— but not the old hag, who cackled with undisguised glee.

Fargo faced the others. "Be a while before your 'he-dog' here plays with whips again. He ain't worth dying for, so just sit still until we're gone. I'll pop over the first mother's son who opens that door."

"You kidding, stranger?" one brave soul spoke up. "That was a tonic to watch."

"Next time drinks're on the house," the old crone added as Fargo stepped out into the desert blast furnace.

* * *

About the same time that Fargo was pulling teeth in the Scorpion's Lair, Mad Dog Barton and his cronies were hotly arguing in the Busted Flat mine.

"Damnitall anyhow, Taffy," Mad Dog said. "Do you ever smell what you're shovelin'? Didn't we just plow all this ground yesterday? I never said we'd kill Fargo last night, only that we needed to start looking for him nights. And we musta got close if he was able to jump us."

The Welshman swore. "He coulda been anywhere when he spotted us. Next time he might not miss."

"Hell, since when do you get ice in your boots the minute somebody chucks lead at us? We stood up to Texas Rangers at the Sabine River."

"Ain't just the shootin'," Taffy insisted. "It's the money we're losing here. No stagecoaches to rob, no federal paymasters, not even a circuit preacher with pass-the-hat money. I ain't had me a woman since we got here—Fargo's hoggin' the only one."

Mad Dog snorted. "You think me and Pepe got one stashed away, chucklehead? We use the poor man's harem just like you do—imagination and the palm of our hand. If we leave before Fargo and the bitch are killed, we're worm fodder."

Pepe Lopez sat in the entrance of the mine shaft, keeping watch as usual. Suddenly he swore in Spanish, *"Madre de Dios!"*

Mad Dog and Taffy cleared leather and raced toward the entrance.

"What's up?" Mad Dog demanded. "Do you see Fargo? Or is it Fenton finally getting here?"

But Pepe, who could read some English, was not looking out across the wavering desert landscape. He was glancing at a creased and seamed newspaper called the *High Desert Observer*, which the gang had purchased in the town of Yucca Canyon on the rim of the Mojave Desert.

"Look," he told both men, handing Mad Dog the newspaper. *"Ay, caramba!* It is the same woman."

"What woman?" Mad Dog demanded. Then he and Taffy spotted the column-wide sketch at the same moment, under a headline that read FIRED MAID REVEALS BOSTON FAMILY'S DEATH VALLEY SECRET.

"I'll be a two-tailed rat catcher!" Mad Dog exclaimed. "It's the sketchin' bitch! You can't tell her hair color, but that's her face, all right, sure as the squitters."

"I don't read too good," Taffy said. "What, is the sketchin' bitch the fired maid?"

Mad Dog, already busy reading, shook his head. "Nah. The maid's back in Boston. She got the boot for stealin' from a family named Winslowe. The sketchin' bitch is Rena Collins, an artist who was playin' hide-the-sausage with George Winslowe, head of the family. Hold off, let me finish the story."

Mad Dog's yellow eyes began to glow with avarice as he read farther down the column. He finished reading and stared at Taffy.

"Finally, the fog lifts," Barton exulted. "I *knew* that high-hattin' slut couldn't be here just to make drawings."

"Chew it a little finer," Taffy insisted.

"Pard, you was just complainin' how we're losin' money hanging around here. But this woman is the key to a fortune in jewels."

Mad Dog recounted the story of George and Marianne Winslowe's only daughter, newlywed Kathrine and her railroad tycoon husband. Part of the infamous Death Valley Party of 1849, they had headed for the coast of California so he could place an early bid for the new state's first railroad contract.

"They never made it outta here," Mad Dog continued. "But the woman and her husband managed to hide the jewels, family heirlooms. The father ain't talkin' 'bout none of this, but the maid claims the jewels are worth at least one hundred thousand dollars."

Taffy and Pepe both goggled at the amount. "God-*damn*!" Taffy exclaimed. "Take us five years to heist that much."

Mad Dog nodded. "Here's the main mile—nobody knows exactly where they're hid, but the maid swears she listened at keyholes, and George Winslowe had a clue his girl sent in a letter mailed after she died. And the Collins woman managed to honey-talk it out of him before she disappeared."

Taffy whistled. "Dante's View! Good chance they didn't

go up there for a look-see of Death Valley but to find the sparklers!"

"Yeah, but did they find them?"

"If they did," Pepe chimed in, "why would they remain in this *desierto*, waiting for us to kill them? *Por Dios*, I would go spend my money."

"Makes sense," Mad Dog agreed. "Boys, we don't dare kill that bitch now—she's got the keys to the mint. But we *do* keep a close eye on her. And you know damn good and well Fargo and her are goin' shares on that loot—she needs his help to survive now that we've planted her guards. So we got two good reasons to kill him, and the sooner the better."

11

Skye Fargo seldom found himself at a loss for a plan, but right now his enemies had him stymied. By day it would be nearly impossible to sneak up on the Barton gang, and by night he couldn't be sure they wouldn't find Rena and Scotty while Fargo was across the valley hunting them down.

"Right now it's a Mexican standoff," he told his two companions that afternoon as they prepared a spartan meal in the shack. "I guess the big idea now is to let them find us and just have it out. These hounds been on us long enough."

They had pounded the mesquite into meal that made a sweet, nourishing gruel similar to cornmeal mush. Rena wouldn't touch the sardines, but Fargo and Scotty planned to use them as bets in poker.

"You know, Skye," Rena said as she worked a horn comb through her hair, "long as we've got time on our hands, why not climb up to the caverns again? Why should the jewels go wasting up there?" She flashed him a coy smile. "Of course it would be equal shares—my father would insist on rewarding you."

Scotty gave that a hoot. "Your father, my sweet aunt! Skye, her beguilin' smile don't fool me none—she's crooked as cat shit."

"Go to blazes, you old drunk," she snapped. "You were much more bearable when you were constantly pickled. This is between me and Skye."

"Where the *hell* do you get that noise? Everybody else is just spokes in the wheel and you're the hub, huh?"

"Both of you whack the cork," Fargo said, picking up

his Henry. Since the close call last night he was being ever vigilant. As he started outside Scotty added: "It's God's truth! She's a velvet sledgehammer. You and me got our tails in a crack on accounta her, and she don't give a frog's fat ass."

"Oh, botheration," Rena dismissed him. "How about it, Skye? Just one more visit, and we could both be rich."

"Rich? I thought those jewels were family heirlooms," he reminded her.

"They are. It's a manner of speaking."

Fargo grinned. "Then let's just leave 'em for the family that owns 'em."

Fargo moved out into the broiling sun from hell, wove his way through the screening rocks, and stopped out in the open valley, forced to squint from the salt desert reflection. He had brought his field glasses with him and grounded his rifle to take a close look in every direction.

Nothing approached from the Panamints to the west nor from the south behind him. But when he looked due north, toward the upper end of Death Valley and Grapevine Canyon beyond it, something dark in the sand caught his eye.

"Damn," he muttered. "Is that what I think it is?"

The object was several miles out, greatly distorted by rippling heat waves, and Fargo didn't trust his own conclusions.

"Scotty!" he shouted. "Rena! C'mon out here, wouldja?"

When they had both joined him, Fargo handed the glasses to each in turn. "Tell me what you see near the mouth of the canyon."

"Looks like a body," Scotty said, surrendering the glasses to Rena. "Or maybe a pile of rags."

"It's not rags," sharp-eyed Rena corrected him. "It's a woman. Looks like she's wearing a dark broadcloth skirt and a coal-shovel bonnet. Also a blue-knitted shawl."

"Horsefeathers!" Scotty jibed. "What would a woman be doin' in Death Valley by her lonesome? Ain't ord'nary, that's for sure. It's a trap, Skye, like when the Sioux stuff a buckskin suit with grass. Mad Dog's gang is baitin' us out."

Fargo nodded, his eyes suddenly grave. "Seems likely, old son. Problem is, when we were up on the rim this morning, I noticed a wagon with a broken singletree. She *could* be a survivor, I s'pose."

Scotty looked less sure of himself. "Sure could be. More folks are takin' this route to avoid extra weeks up in the Sierras. She mighta crawled down here to find water in the canyon."

Fargo speared his fingers through his hair, mulling it.

"I'd lay odds on a trap," he admitted. "But so what if it is? The two of us are going to have to face Barton and his curs in a lead-chuckin' contest sooner or later, and three of them against two of us ain't bad odds."

Fargo pointed at the wild jumble of boulders well behind the shack. "Rena, get horsed and go hide back there. Don't come out until I give you the hail."

All three tacked their mounts, Fargo and Scotty heading toward Grapevine Canyon while Rena went into deep hiding. Fargo's vigilant eyes stayed in constant scanning motion.

"Wish now I had me a long gun," Scotty remarked.

"My Henry's worth two rifles," Fargo boasted. "I'll take all the long shots. You just hold your powder for targets that get within thirty yards or so. Stay frosty and don't squeeze that trigger until you know you can score. Only the shots that hit matter."

They drew closer to the shape in the sand.

"Looks like a woman, all right," Fargo confirmed. "Looks mighty dead, too."

Even so, Fargo's god-fear was back, itching like a new scab. Both men swung down and quickly hobbled their mounts. Fargo walked closer, dropped to one knee, and lifted the bonnet aside.

"We been hornswoggled!" Scotty exclaimed.

The pox-scarred face of the "woman" lying on the ground belonged to the same bully boy Fargo had roughed up that morning at the Scorpion's Lair—only now there was a neat bullet hole in his forehead, no doubt put there by the Barton gang after they hatched this new scheme to bait out their quarry.

"The death hug's a-comin'!" Scotty roared out even as a withering crackle of gunfire opened up on them.

The Barton gang attacked from the direction of the sun, Comanche style. They had patiently waited in the mouth of the canyon and now surged out from the boulders, coming like the devil beating bark.

Fargo pulled Scotty down with him. "This is easy pick-in's, old son," the Trailsman assured him. "A prone position is the best. Just hold and squeeze."

Lead peppered both men, kicking up geysers of rock salt and whistling close to the Ovaro and Scotty's mule. The bullet-wise stallion would stand in place, Fargo knew, but it was imperative to keep the attackers back so they didn't shoot the animals.

"Katy Christ, Skye!" a nervous Scotty said. "The hell you waitin' for? Christmas? Air 'em out!"

The highly disciplined Trailsman, however, was waiting for sure hits. He levered the Henry, tossed the butt of the stock into his shoulder, and drew a bead on the man astride the reddish-gold California sorrel, John "Mad Dog" Barton. The Henry kicked solidly into Fargo's shoulder, and Mad Dog's hat went spinning off.

Next bullet curls your toes, Fargo vowed, levering again.

And then disaster struck—B. Tyler Henry's ejector mechanism, which usually functioned with the flawless clicking of a roulette wheel, suddenly jammed, a brass casing wedged in the ejector port. Despite all Fargo's efforts at constant cleaning and oiling, the merciless sand and grit and wind of Death Valley had caused a stoppage. Fargo took immediate action to clear it, but the stubborn casing would not come out without disassembly.

The trio pounded closer, long guns spitting fire and death.

"Holy Hannah, Skye!" Scotty screeched. "Any closer and they'll be kissin' us good-bye! Waltz it to 'em, boy!"

"My rifle's jammed. Give 'em a few pop shots, Scotty!"

Fargo skinned back his Colt and both men let loose, a few shots whizzing in close enough to turn the gang. However, they realized Fargo's famous Henry was out of the fight, and they re-formed for a second charge.

"Shit," Fargo swore, rapidly opening the loading gate and thumbing six more beans into the wheel of his Colt. "Now they know they can plug our mounts."

"T'hell with this," Scotty muttered, kneecaps popping as he jumped up.

"We can't retreat," Fargo snapped. "They'll shoot us to rag tatters before we get the hobbles off!"

Scotty ignored him, racing toward his mule. The attackers thundered closer, rifles whip-cracking.

"Heads up!" Scotty shouted behind him, and Fargo glanced up just in time to see a can of blasting powder coming at him.

Fargo caught it with his left hand, realizing that a fuse was out of the question and there was only one way—a slim chance at best—to detonate the black powder. He did a quick border shift, flipping his Colt to his left hand, the can to his right.

Fargo waited another two seconds, bullets blurring the air around him, then tossed the can out in a high arc. He flipped his six-gun back to his right hand and took the best aim he could on the falling can. When it was about the same height as the mounted men, Fargo snapped off a round.

The resulting explosion echoed its way down the long valley, and the sound bounced back and forth between the sheer rock escarpments on both sides. It was too far from the men to do serious damage, but their thoroughly spooked horses took off in three separate directions, ignoring the commands of their blast-shaken riders.

Fargo whooped, scooping up Scotty and spinning him around as if they were dancing. "You wily old sourdough, I could kiss you! You just saved both our lives."

"You done it," Scotty insisted. "Slick, I ain't *never* seen shootin' like that! Them egg-suckin' varmints didn't know what hit 'em."

"Let's raise dust before they ride back here and finish the job. First thing I'm doing is getting this Henry repaired," Fargo vowed as he untied the Ovaro's rawhide hobbles. "Once these plug-uglies shake it off, they'll be back with a vengeance."

Fargo didn't worry too much, during the ride south to the shack, about his enemies spotting them. The Barton gang would have bigger problems getting their horses under control—Fargo had seen panicked mounts run themselves to death before a rider could regain mastery. More than one cavalry officer had been forced to shoot his own mount from under him to avoid going over a cliff.

"Didja see Mad Dog's beard?" Scotty crowed. "Son of a bitch caught fire! That'll learn him to ruin *my* beard, the coyote-ugly sidewinder."

"Rena!" Fargo called out when they reined in out front of the hidden shack. "Rena, all clear!"

Dead silence greeted his hail.

"Rena! Sing out, girl!"

Only a hollow shrieking of wind in the rocks. On a sudden hunch, Fargo raised his eyes past the wild jumble of boulders ahead to the steep slope of the Funeral Mountains that bordered much of the east wall of Death Valley.

"That *stupid* little greenhorn," Fargo burst out. "She's tryin' to get up to those caverns."

Rena, astride her chestnut, was attempting to negotiate a steep, rocky slope about one-third of the way up the face of a mountain.

"She can't make it, can she?" Scotty asked.

"Hell no. Not even on foot. I mapped those mountains myself, and the only way up is the slope we took well north of here—the divide between the Black and Funeral Mountains that leads to Dante's View. She's on a fool's errand."

"Even if she did somehow miracle her ass up there," Scotty added, "she'd still have miles to go due north 'fore she reached that bottleneck. With no trail to follow."

"That's the straight," Fargo agreed. "C'mon, let's try to shout her down before Barton's gang spots her. I'm not risking my horse for that damned fool. I'm all for protecting a woman, but this one hasn't got the brains God gave a rabbit. Those damn 'family heirlooms' are gonna send her to an early grave. Maybe us, too."

Both men led their mounts behind the shack and ground-reined them. They cupped their hands around their mouths and bellowed to catch her attention. Rena looked down, spotting them, and waved. But she continued her steep ascent.

"Bleedin' Holy Ghost!" Scotty cursed. "She's about to fall bass ackwards off that mountain!"

A moment later, however, it was the mountain that fell backward. Rena's chestnut dislodged a large rock, the rock dislodged more rocks, and suddenly the entire slope beneath her heaved into motion.

"Rockslide!" Fargo shouted, spinning around on his heel. "Grab your mule and get out onto the valley floor. It's all headed our way!"

Rena was past worrying about now as Fargo and Scotty

scrambled to save their own hides. The ground beneath their feet shook and vibrated as if an earthquake had struck, and they could hear the accumulating roar as more and more rocks and boulders were swept up in the rush.

Fargo sent a cross-shoulder glance behind him as he ran out into the valley, leading the Ovaro.

"Christ, don't stop!" he shouted at Scotty. "It's coming into the valley!"

Moments later the tumult swept both men up in a thick, choking cloud of rock salt, and Fargo felt his stomach turn to a ball of ice as tons of dangerous, hurtling rock, ranging from fist-sized to house-sized, bounced, rolled, and flew past them. Fargo tried to use his stallion as a buffer, but in the blind, choking confusion only sheer luck would save him or Scotty.

Finally came the blessed sound of the slide tapering off. But the dust cloud lingered in the furnace heat like heavy fog.

"Scotty!" Fargo shouted. "You still among the living?"

"I must be," his quavering voice replied. "But I pissed my pants, Skye. I guess Rena finally copped it, huh?"

Fargo coughed from the dust coating his throat. "Unless she managed to stay above it. In which case I'm gonna fan her britches until her ass turns into kindling. Let's see if the shack survived."

Astoundingly, it had. The east wall was crumpled in two places, but the bulk of the structure remained intact—in fact was even better hidden.

More of the choking dust blew away, and Fargo didn't credit his own eyes when he glanced up the slope: Rena, obviously white and shaken, was on her way down, she and her horse evidently unharmed.

"Skye!" she called out as she picked her way through the rocks and boulders. "Are you and Scotty all right?"

"What is wrong with you?" Scotty sputtered. "And what doctor told you so?"

Fargo did a slow boil. "Oh, hell, don't worry about us—*we* don't mind dying just so long as you find those jewels."

"If you'd just help me," she replied archly, "we'd have them by—*oh!*"

Fargo plucked her off the chestnut, sat down on a boulder, and threw her across his lap. True to his word, he spanked her round little derriere with force and energy.

"Skye! *Skye!* Stop it! That hurts! Oh, *stop* it, I said! That's too hard!"

"Next time you pull a jackass stunt like that," he promised as he finally turned her loose, his right hand stinging, "I'm just going to shoot you. You saw what Mad Dog Barton did to the Conways. What makes you think he'll go any easier on you?"

12

Fargo's Henry, it turned out, was in worse shape than simply jammed at the ejector port. The brass shell casing had warped in the fiery sun and bent the ejector rod.

At first the Trailsman feared the weapon was ruined beyond repair, leaving them at the mercy of three ruthless killers with long guns. But he spent an entire day in a delicate repair job, using the Sibley stove as a makeshift forge, and by evening of the following day his repeating rifle had a new braze, but functioned flawlessly.

When he wasn't working on the Henry, Fargo kept a close eye on the surrounding valley. And he definitely did not like what he was seeing.

"Mad Dog is playing ring-around-the-rosy with us," he announced to Rena and Scotty.

Scotty's dour face slid into a frown. He had been forced to leave the Scorpion's Lair before he could plank his cash for a bottle. Since then he'd been a sore-tailed bear.

"You'll have to spell it out plain, Skye," he replied. "You sound like Rena when you take the long way around the barn."

"You act like I'm the criminal, Scotty," Rena complained. "It's Mad Dog's gang who are the villains, remember?"

"Ain't sayin' you're a criminal," Scotty retorted. "But look at yestiddy, you startin' that slide—you're a dagger at our throats, you little hussy."

"*Both* of you pipe down," Fargo snapped. "I'll keep it clear as ice: The gang have changed their tactics. I know for a fact they know our location now. But they're holding back."

"How you know that?" Scotty demanded.

"Because I've spotted them through the field glasses, and they're studying this exact spot."

Scotty nodded. "All because of that calico rose's damn fool notions."

"You don't own me," she fired back. "I don't have to follow orders."

"Whoopie doodle! Ain't none of us joined at the hip," Scotty reminded her. "You don't like followin' orders, cut loose."

Rena clamped her teeth rather than retort.

"Like I was saying." Fargo took over again. "They're just content to watch us now. But until yesterday they were itching to find us and kill us. Why the change?"

"Afraid of you," Scotty suggested. "That blasting powder damn near took off their eyebrows."

"And you killed their friend, the one called Kid," Rena reminded him. "They're just leery."

Fargo shook his head. "These boys are used to cutting up rough, and they're no cowards. No, they've got reasons for changing their tactics. After dark I'm going to break this stalemate and locate their hideout."

Fargo had no intention of leaving Scotty and Rena alone in the shack. When the night was well advanced he led them to their first campsite on the valley floor. A rising moon lighted the very tips of the surrounding mountains with a silver patina.

"Scotty's in charge," Fargo said bluntly, staring at Rena. "Forget those damn jewels, hear? They ain't worth a shinplaster to a dead woman. I want both of you right here, hiding in the circle of boulders."

"I've learned my lesson," she promised him in the ghostly moonlight.

Scotty groaned. "Yeah, sure. And pigs don't snort, neither."

Rena lifted her chin in defiance at Scotty. "I promise, Skye. Don't worry about me."

Fargo said nothing to this, although in fact her word wasn't worth a busted tug chain. Before he rode out, he took the prospector aside. "Damn it, Scotty, *watch* her. If she heads up to that bottleneck again, she's on her own."

Scotty nodded. "She ain't like most of the homely-lonely

gals you see out west. But she's so full of shit her feet are sliding. I'm damned if I'm gonna wet-nurse that woman. Keep your nose to the wind, Skye."

Fargo had a good idea where the hideout must be, but he approached it from the most oblique angle possible, hugging the shadows at the base of the Panamints. He also tied off his Ovaro well north of the suspected hideout, leaving him in the piles of scree and proceeding on foot.

Again and again Fargo ducked behind the screening boulders, searching for a camp. And suddenly his patience was rewarded: He rounded a huge pile of ore tailings and spotted the headframe of a mine, oily yellow lantern light leaking from the entrance.

Fargo knocked the riding thong from the hammer of his Colt and loosened his long, narrow-bladed Arkansas toothpick in its boot sheath. For a few minutes he cautiously studied the darkness, searching for a sentry. Then, catfooted, he crept closer to the mine entrance.

He heard voices before he saw anyone. "—maybe she *has* cut Fargo in on the deal, but I'll guarandamntee you they ain't found the jewels yet. They'd've snuck out of Death Valley by now."

Mad Dog Barton. So here, finally, was the den of cutthroats. Fargo rose to peek from behind a pile of slag and spotted him about forty feet into the mine shaft, in conversation with the redhead Fargo had wounded in the leg—conversation, Fargo was shocked to learn, that centered around the same jewels Rena was bound and determined to lay hands on. So the gang's plans had indeed changed.

"That all depends," the redhead argued. "We know Fargo buried the Conways—and in this heat, too. What if the family was friends of his? From what I hear of him, Fargo is the type to hang around and avenge the killings."

Fargo had a better view of the two men. On the frontier a man could wear one revolver, or none, but two was either a grandstander or a killer. Both these two-gun men were definitely killers.

"The woman," Mad Dog said. "The newspaper story called her Rena Collins. She's just a fancy whore who got the details by lettin' a married man top her. She's got no right to them jewels, and you can bet your sweet ass *she* ain't hangin' around once she gets 'em."

Fargo tried to position himself better, hoping for a clear shot. He could clearly see Barton's ivory-and-silver revolvers in a richly embroidered sash. Obviously he fancied himself an outlaw fashion plate. Besides the sash and a brocaded vest, he wore fancy calfskin boots with two-inch heels. But a scattergun was propped up on either side of him, discouraging Fargo from rushing the men. Nor could he get a clear shot from outside—three sore-used horses, all carrying a different brand over the left hip, kept shifting and blocking Fargo's targets. They would sound a warning the moment he went in.

The horses . . . Where, Fargo wondered again, was the Mexican?

"One thing's for sure," the redhead said as he took out the makings, crimped a paper, and shook some tobacco into it. "We ain't gonna roll our blankets unless they do. And we ain't gonna lay hands on that blond bitch until we kill Fargo."

Fargo watched him pinch the ends of his quirly and twist it into a smoke. He unbuckled his spurs and crossed his legs at the ankles, lighting a phosphor on his tooth and touching fire to the cigarette.

"Way I see it, Taffy," Mad Dog said, yellow eyes gleaming, "when you can't raise the bridge, you lower the river."

"Never mind the parlor riddles," Taffy snapped. "Spell that out."

"I mean Fenton, you soft brain. Fargo's never laid eyes on him, and you know Fenton Kinney can con the balls off a stud bull."

"Yeah, but that long stretch in jail coulda changed him. We need our own plan."

Fargo thought he heard a distant footstep behind him, but he dared not leave now—a plan was being hatched.

"All right, Furnace Creek is the only water I know of in Death Valley," Mad Dog elaborated. "What if the three of us just plant ourselves next to it, like squatters, and force Fargo's hand? He'll have to shoot it out with us to use it."

Another footstep, and this time Fargo heard the whispered words, "*Un beso*, eh?"

Just a little kiss . . . Fargo whirled around just in the nick of time to see a twirling object streaking toward him.

*   *   *

93

Fargo's survival instincts had been honed in scores of deadly scrapes, and it was not his way to slow down his reactions by thinking about them first. Instantly he tucked and rolled, feeling a white-hot wire of pain across his back as a throwing blade sliced into him.

He rocked up onto his heels, Henry at the ready. Generous moonlight showed the Mexican standing atop a boulder, his face obscured by the flat-crowned sombrero. Rope-soled sandals had allowed him to move in close. A raw-wool serape was folded over one shoulder.

Fargo immediately realized his dilemma: If he shot the Mexican, he would sign his own death warrant. The man laughed softly.

"See how it is, Fargo? But do not worry—I will not warn them, either. This will be a contest of blades, and *no* man has ever beat Pepe Lopez in a knife fight. Tonight, gringo, you cross over. And I become the man who killed the *famoso* Trailsman."

Even as Fargo dropped his Henry and snatched the Arkansas toothpick from his boot, Lopez leaped down toward him. The Mexican had learned early on that no move in a knife fight could be wasted, and that each move should do double duty. So as his weight slammed into Fargo he brought his left forearm up into the frontiersman's neck, while his knife hand made a fast, direct thrust toward Fargo's torso.

Instantly Fargo weighed all the dangers and focused on stopping just one for the moment—the deadly blade of a ten-inch bowie. Even as the Mexican's momentum knocked him backward, left arm snapping his head back even harder, Fargo grabbed for his opponent's right wrist.

He caught it, yanked the Mexican into the direction of their momentum, and then relaxed his muscles for the impact. Even as they whammed into the hard, shale-littered ground, the Mexican began fighting.

He was like the very Wendigo himself, Fargo thought with stunned amazement. The Mexican writhed, kicked, bit. To Fargo, trapped beneath the whirling dervish and trying to get his breath back, it felt like five men were on him. He gave a mighty heave of his back, and the two combatants were rolling and bouncing through piles of rocks and slag and scree.

"I see blood!" Lopez gloated. "This feels good on your back, *verdad*?"

Indeed, Fargo barely restrained himself from roaring out like a burned bear, for the pain was instant and harsh. They rolled some more, colliding with rocks over and over, first Fargo, then Lopez. They rolled over jagged rocks and shards of flint that dug bloody gobbets of flesh from both men's bodies.

"Un brazo fuerte," Lopez taunted, meaning the deadly embrace they were locked in. Fargo's weaker left hand gripped his opponent's knife hand at the wrist, and the Mexican's left arm blocked Fargo from making the killing thrust.

"I will bull your woman after I kill you," Lopez taunted, breathing hard through clenched teeth. "She will cry out like a queen in heat and marvel at my size, for she has judged all men by you whites."

Fargo recognized the strategy: Lopez was seeking to rattle his adversary, to throw Fargo off guard through a burst of anger by a constant string of vile epithets and filthy insults. But the Trailsman refused to rise to the bait. Instead, as he struggled he began to grin—the goading, unnerving grin that silently defied any man to make him whimper.

That might have been a mistake, Fargo realized a heartbeat later, when Lopez found new strength. His knife hand suddenly drove closer, bringing the point of his blade close enough to prick Fargo's flesh.

"Do you feel it, gringo devil?" Lopez tormented him. "Do you feel where my blade is? *Ay, Dios!* Poised between the fourth and fifth ribs. From there it is a straight, easy thrust into the warm and beating heart."

Fargo was already well aware of that, but he remained silent. All these sustained insults and curses were wasting valuable wind Lopez would need for the fight. Sure enough, when he paused to gasp for air Fargo made his move. He arched his back quick and hard, throwing the Mexican clear.

As they came to their feet, each man's breath was blowing and snorting like a played-out pack animal's. Seeing the Mexican, bruised and battered, leap back into action was impressive. Now Lopez went all out for a fast, furious, flashy kill.

Still taunting his opponent, the Mexican slashed rapidly and repeatedly, relentless in his advance, like a swarm of wasps. His method was brutal and direct: Overwhelm his opponent, wait until he was rattled and dropped his defense, then make the killing thrust.

But Fargo, who lacked flash and speed, firmly believed that "slow and steady wins the race." While Lopez taunted and twirled, Fargo instinctively stuck to a cold, calm, lethal patience, waiting for the moment that he knew would come.

"Your head I will pickle in a jar and charge others to see," the Mexican goaded. "I will make a parfleche from your manhood and give it to my favorite grandmother. A necklace from your teeth will earn credit at any trading post. I will not waste one part of the great legend after I carve you up."

As he said this last word, Lopez drove forward and slashed, opening a long slice across Fargo's chest. White-hot pain licked at him, but this time the Trailsman surprised his more nimble opponent—he feinted left, lunged right, and took a strip of hide off Lopez's left thigh.

Not only did this induce a harsh grunt of pain from Fargo's enemy, but it shook his swaggering confidence. For he was discovering that Fargo was in fact close to his own skill at knife fighting—a combat art at which Mexican men excelled. The gringo had a long, strong reach and a remarkably unerring eye as well as the reflexes and timing of a cat, though he was not as fancy as Lopez, did not own so many moves or hazard such dazzling footwork.

Fargo waited patiently, biding his time. Common sense told him that each one of Lopez's dazzling movements invited a mistake. And finally it came.

Lopez feinted left but placed his propelling foot on loose shale. His legs slid out from under him and he went down hard. Fargo leaped on him, and one hand gripped the Mexican's chin to expose the neck; his knife hand slashed hard and deep, opening the throat up like a cheese. Lopez quickly drowned in his own blood.

Fargo's trembling legs gave out and he collapsed, exhausted. It seemed a miracle that sounds of the fight hadn't drawn the other two out. Fargo was too worn out now to face a pair of draw-shoot killers.

As he gathered strength to return to his horse, Fargo recalled the talk inside the cave—talk about taking over the water hole. His lips twitched into a grin as a plan occurred to him. They wanted Furnace Creek, did they? Then Fargo would make sure they got it.

"This ain't the first time that sneaky greaser has prowled all night," Mad Dog Barton said as he threw the saddle onto his sorrel and centered it.

Taffy grunted affirmation. The new morning sun was a giant gold coin balanced atop the Funeral Mountains across the valley. "Hell, I don't mind him prowling around—keeps us safer. But he was s'posed to come back last night and rub down the horses."

"Unless," Mad Dog suggested, "he ran into Fargo."

"Ain't likely. Pepe's like a shadow after dark. He'll turn up. Let's water these horses and see if we can find him."

Both men led their mounts out into the stifling heat and forked leather. As they bore north toward the mouth of Grapevine Canyon they kept a nervous eye out for Fargo.

They entered the canyon and headed toward the upper plateau, where Furnace Creek never ran dry.

Mad Dog abruptly reined in. "What in pluperfect hell? Is that Pepe waitin' for us?"

Both men squinted to see better in the dry, hot haze. Just ahead, Pepe Lopez sat with his back to a boulder, sombrero pulled low over his face.

"Sure is," Taffy said. "The crazy son of a bitch is asleep. C'mon, let's roust him out."

"Wait just a goddamn minute," Mad Dog said. "His horse is back in the mine. How the hell did he get here?"

"Yeah," Taffy said. "And *why* would he be here without his horse? It's a long walk."

Both men shucked out a short gun and rode cautiously toward the shallow, gravel-bed creek.

"Pepe!" Mad Dog shouted. "*Arriba*, you crazy chilipep! *Que pasa?*"

"Mad Dog," Taffy said, swinging down and holding his horse's bridle, "he ain't asleep. He's either dead drunk or just dead."

Taffy knocked the tilted sombrero off to reveal Pepe's neck sliced open from ear to ear, so deep the head was in danger of breaking off. The sight shocked them like a hard slap in the face. Both men glanced nervously around.

"Looks like there's a note tucked into his belt," Mad Dog said, swinging a leg over the cantle and joining his sole remaining partner.

He unfolded an old reward dodger and read the printing on the back: " 'I like your idea about seizing the water hole, Mad Dog. So I put Lopez on first watch.' "

Mad Dog turned fish-belly white.

"Is that all he wrote?" Taffy demanded.

Mad Dog shook his head. "Not quite. It's signed, 'Skye Fargo, a friend of the Conways.' "

13

Fargo had said very little, after returning to the shack the night before, about what he'd overheard in the abandoned mine. The cuts on his back and chest needed tending, and shortly afterward he fell asleep, exhausted. But as the three of them shared a breakfast of mesquite bread and tepid water, he again mulled over what those jewels were doing to Mad Dog's greedy mind.

"What's wrong, Skye?" Rena asked him. "You're miles away."

"I'm right here," he assured her. "And guess what? The whole damn country knows *you're* here, too."

She started and looked at him across the trestle table. "Surely you jest?"

"Do I look like I'm laughing? Seems that George Winslowe, the married fellow you were . . . ah, keeping company with back in Boston, fired his maid for stealing. She's not too happy about it and she's been flappin' her gums to the newspapers, and the whole story—the *real* story—is out. I heard the gang talking about it last night."

Rena turned marble white. "They know? But that's impossible!"

"Believe it or not, some criminals can read." Fargo repeated everything he'd heard, and when Rena realized the gang did indeed know about the jewels, worry molded her face.

"It's all true," she admitted. "That damned maid—Babette! She was jealous when George spurned her advances. And she was always spying on us."

"You're a good one to talk," Scotty growled. "Diddling a married man, yet actin' so high and mighty with us. It's

99

true I don't amount up to much, and once I was even jugged for cutting timber on government land. But you're prac'ly a grave robber."

"Never mind the moral lecture," Fargo snapped. "The main thing is, what will Barton do?"

"She shoulda told us everything," Scotty persisted.

"More than a quibble, less than a quarrel," Rena insisted. "Giving you all the details wouldn't have changed anything."

"What I heard last night," Fargo said, "that's all of it?"

"Yes."

"Hand to God?"

"I swear it on the bones of my mother."

"What about the guards?" Fargo pressed. "Were they cronies?"

"No, they were real. I told Allan Pinkerton I needed protection while looking for my sister's grave. I was going to cut them in once we found the jewels."

"Christ on a cracker!" Scotty exploded. "All that horse crap about your sister and your rich daddy that publishes a magazine."

"Why am *I* suddenly the archvillain of the piece?" Rena demanded. "All right, so I'm a scavenger. But I didn't kill Deputy Conway and his family."

Fargo stood up and buckled on his heavy leather gun belt. "Rena's right, her not being square with us didn't matter much. Mad Dog figures he has to kill us—all of us— eventually on account we know about the rubout of the Conways. But first he means to capture Rena and torture her for the location of the jewels."

Fargo clapped on his broad-brimmed plainsman's hat and continued. "But what Mad Dog plans don't matter a hill of beans to me. You'll find no six-pointed stars in Death Valley. If there's to be law, we're it. And there *will* be law. Let's get horsed."

Out back, the Ovaro bumped his nose against Fargo's chest in greeting.

"Hey-up, old campaigner," Fargo said, scratching the stallion's withers. "You'll be tanking up soon."

He tossed on the blanket, pad, and saddle, cinching the pinto loose in the oven heat. The Ovaro took the bit easily when Fargo slipped the bridle on.

"There might be trouble in Grapevine Canyon," he warned his companions. "Mad Dog was making noise last night about camping out beside the Furnace Creek water hole from now on."

"Damn," Scotty said. "Looks like the showdown might be here."

"Not likely," Fargo said as they rode out into the flat, glaring valley. "The plan is stupid. There's other water around here if you know where to find it. Besides—I left a little surprise to take the vinegar out of 'em."

When Fargo described what he'd done with the body of Pepe Lopez, even Rena broke into a grin.

"Serves them right," she opined. "After what I witnessed in that cabin, nothing is too low for them."

"With the beaner dead," Scotty added, "it's down to Barton and that redhead with the accent. 'Course, them two looks the most dangersome. Two-gun men."

"Stone-hearted killers," Fargo agreed, keeping his lake blue eyes in constant motion. "Mad Dog, they say, is quicker than eyesight in a draw-shoot."

"How quick are you, Skye?" Rena asked.

"He's quicker than thought," Scotty answered.

"That's saloon gossip," Fargo scoffed. "So far I been quick enough to stay alive, but I do my damnedest to avoid slapping leather. All it takes is one factory-made cartridge to malfunction, and I'm headed beyond the mountains."

Fargo led them into the canyon. As usual, to avoid a possible ambush from the cabin, they rode wide on the east flank. By now, as they headed toward the upper plateau and Furnace Creek, Fargo had his Henry out of its boot and Scotty tugged his black-gripped Remington from his belt.

"No sign of those two sidewinders," Scotty remarked as they bore down on the water hole. "And I don't see the Mexer's body neither. Looks like you scared the snot outta them, Skye."

Fargo, however, was tacking up no bunting. Something was wrong—it was a mere premonitory pulsation more than certain knowledge, for as yet the glare up ahead made it hard to see.

Moments later he did spot something, and his scalp began to tingle.

Rena gasped. "All the saints! Skye, is that what I think it is?"

He nodded, his voice failing him. In the same place, and position, where he'd left Pepe Lopez now sat Matt Conway's body. The sons of bitches had dug it up to pay Fargo back in his own coin.

The desert dryness had left the body only slightly decomposed. All three stared at the grisly sight of pale, silent death.

"I feel like hell," Fargo admitted. "It's my fault. I thought it was funny, leaving the Mexican to scare them. Thought it might rattle them into making a mistake. I underestimated them, but I won't do it again."

With the resilience of a frontier survivor, Fargo shook it off. "C'mon, let's water the horses. Then I'm going to bury Matt a second time. If they touch that grave again, I won't just kill them—I'll skin them alive and salt the exposed meat."

Finding Conway's body was only the beginning of the shocking sacrilege. When the trio returned to the cabin, Fargo vigilant for an ambush, they discovered Marsha and Juliet Conway had been dragged from the common grave and hacked to pieces.

"This'll cost them dear," was all a grim-faced Fargo remarked before he reburied the family.

Fargo was on the horns of a dilemma: He knew where Barton and his partner were staying, and they knew where he was. He preferred to take the attack to them first, but Mad Dog's top priority was those jewels, which meant seizing Rena. So the only choice was to let them attack.

"They want this over as bad as we do," Fargo told his companions that evening as the sun's hellfire began to wane. "I'd bet my horse they plan to come down on us tonight like all wrath."

Rena watched Fargo run a bore brush down the seven-and-a-half-inch barrel of his Colt. "You don't seem too perturbed by that prospect, Skye."

Fargo followed the bore brush with a wiping patch. "Six-gun persuasion works both ways, and I'm a mighty persuasive fellow."

Scotty snorted. "Damn straight, slick. You've kilt two of them, they've kilt *none* of us."

But superstitious Scotty knocked on the wooden trestle table.

"Ain't just me," Fargo insisted. "When you're sober, Scotty, you're a reliable man. And even this beautiful jewel thief of ours has plenty of sand. We're in a scrape, all right, but if we stay frosty and shoot plumb, I like our chances."

At sundown Scotty stood the first two-hour watch while Fargo tried not to let Rena's seductive smiles and poses sidetrack him from the danger at hand. He felt almost relieved when it was time to spell the prospector.

"Having a good time out here?" he greeted the old-timer out front in the valley.

"Oh, yeah, it's a barrel of monks."

"Any trouble?"

"Mighty quiet," Scotty reported. "But then, so's a graveyard."

Fargo's first watch, too, was uneventful. Around ten p.m. Scotty took over again and Fargo returned to the shack.

"You're not in bed yet?" he asked Rena as he tossed his hat onto the table.

"*Bed* I don't mind, Skye, but I'm too nervous to sleep."

Her eyes and her tone were a clear invitation. She wore a calico skirt and a low-cut *camisola* of the type favored by Mexican women.

"If I was ever tempted," Fargo replied. "But it wouldn't be smart."

Rena showed him a wet cloth. "Well, at least pull off your shirt. Those cuts on your back and chest need bathing."

"They do smart like the dickens," Fargo admitted and surrendered. He tugged off his fringed buckskin shirt and unbuckled his gun belt, leaving it within easy reach of his bunk.

The cloth was soothing and cool, even sensuous, on his injured back. Fargo whiffed the hyacinth smell of her hair, which hung loose and tickled his skin.

"For a handsome man like you," she teased, "each conquest is just one more leaf on the tree, right?"

"I'd build each one a monument if I had the money."

"Huh! You'd need your own mint. Turn over so I can do your chest."

She wiped off his shallow but long cut, leaning so close Fargo felt her moist, animal-warm breath.

"Impressive chest," she told him. "You showed me yours, now I'll show you mine."

In a flash she tugged the *camisola* up, exposing two large, solid breasts that defied gravity by riding so high. The plum-colored nipples begged Fargo's lips to suck them.

"Do you like my *chichonas*? Isn't that what Mexican women call their breasts?"

"Hey," Fargo replied weakly, "I'm *tryin'* to be disciplined tonight."

However, he made no effort to stop her when she opened his fly.

"I see *this* boy's feeling sparky," she teased when his hard shaft, the tip swollen purple, popped up like a hungry predator. "My lands, it's so big it needs reins."

Expertly, Rena wrapped the wet cloth around him and began working it rapidly with both hands like an Indian firedrill. And as if it were indeed a firedrill, Fargo's staff began to glow with erotic heat that pulsed into his sac and groin. The warm, tickling pleasure coaxed a groan from the Trailsman, who had given up any pretext of protesting.

"Let's finish this off proper," she suggested in a husky whisper, hiking her skirt over her flaring hips to reveal a mons bush a shade darker than her strawberry blond hair.

She straddled Fargo on the bunk, reaching down to open her nether lips wider. In the light of a guttering candle Fargo enjoyed a thrilling view of the pink depths of her sex, honey-glazed with desire and radiating the heady odor of female musk.

Rena lined him up with her portal and plunged down onto him, hips gyrating as she took her greedy pleasure. Her talented love muscle squeezed and released, milking him for all the pleasure she could get. Fargo took turns sucking and nibbling on each spearmint-tasting nipple, teasing them stiff.

"Oh, *do* me, Skye!" she begged. "Yes, so deep and nice!"

Several times she cried out as climaxes overwhelmed her, each more explosive than the one before. As her grand peak approached, Fargo had to cup her taut ass in both hands to control the thrashing of her out-of-control body.

"Skye! Skye, my God! Oh—*ohh*—*anhhh*!"

Her carnal explosion triggered his own, and Fargo's body arched like a bow as he made the conclusive thrusts with the urgency and power of a randy stallion.

Completely spent by their unbridled passion, both of them collapsed in a dazed heap of entwined flesh. Sometimes the mazy waltz left Fargo stupefied for countless minutes, and this was one of those times. However, he flew off the bunk, instantly alert, when gunshots split the silence outside.

"Get dressed!" he barked at Rena. "Then get on the floor. And have that derringer ready."

Fargo ignored his buckskin shirt and buckled on his heavy leather gun belt before snatching his Henry off the table. The gunshots from outside were still rapid and fierce and he worried about Scotty. He wondered, briefly, why no bullets were flying into the shack, but now was the time for action, not analysis.

Fargo ignored the hide door, knowing hot lead might pour into him the moment he charged out. Instead, he somersaulted through the back window, taking the last of the oiled paper with him.

Rifle shots rang out, but he could spot no muzzle flash. Staying low in the blue-white moonlight, he headed toward Scotty's position. Bullets whanged off the boulders, whizzing dangerously close to his head.

"Scotty!" he called out. "You still alive?"

"Scared shitless but still sassy!" the prospector's tense voice replied. "Christomighty! I'm pinned down like a bug under a boot!"

Fargo could hear the weaker pops of Scotty's Remington. "Hang on, old campaigner. I'm on my way."

Fargo got an ear location on one of the rifles and opened fire with his Henry. His newly repaired rifle was operating smoothly again, but the 200-grain bullets were a poor match for the 500-grain loads splatting in around him.

Fargo could just make out the prospector straight ahead, sheltered in some of the new boulders that Rena had brought down in the recent rockslide. The Trailsman cast his gaze about in hopes of finding the attackers' horses so

105

he could cut the hobbles off. But the horses, like the men, remained well hidden.

"Coming in!" Fargo told Scotty, turning up a burst of speed to join him in the boulders. This drew a fresh spate of high-powered rifle slugs, forcing both men to duck.

"I can't see muzzle flash," Fargo complained tersely. "But these slugs are coming from the scree due south from here. Since we can't spot our target, we'll have to saturate the area. Make it hot, Scotty!"

As fast as he could work the lever, Fargo emptied the Henry's magazine and immediately skinned back his Colt, adding six more pills to the dose of lead. Scotty tossed the remaining four slugs from his Remington.

"This shooter's quiet now," Fargo said as he snapped open the loading gate of his Colt and thumbed in reloads. "But where's the other one?"

A feminine scream from the shack answered Fargo's question.

"Christ! How hog stupid can I be?" Fargo muttered. "They need Rena to find those jewels."

Before he could leap to Rena's aid, however, a terrifying blast shattered the night. A double load of Blue Whistlers set off sparks when they slammed into the rocks around Fargo and Scotty.

"That would be Mad Dog," Fargo said, recalling the two scatterguns the owlhoot kept close to hand. "So the red-head is in the shack."

He tensed his muscles to try another run, but evidently Mad Dog had a good eye on him. Once again a scattergun roared from both barrels, spraying buckshot on Fargo and Scotty. This time, however, Fargo spotted red-orange muzzle flash.

A sudden shot from the shack was followed by a man's sharp curse.

Aiming for the spot where he'd seen the scattergun belch flame, Fargo spaced out four shots from his short gun as he tore back toward the shack. The hide door slapped open and the redhead appeared in the moonlight, trying to drag Rena out. Forced to caution by darkness and Rena's proximity to her would-be captor, Fargo sent one round whistling close to the man's head.

Startled, he let go of Rena. But before Fargo could pop

him over with his remaining bullet, the two-gun killer proved his skill as a shootist. His right-hand gun seemed to leap into his fist, and if not for the darkness Fargo would have been with his ancestors that very night.

Six times his gun spat fire, forcing the Trailsman to cover down.

"Taffy!" rasped out a desperate voice. "Let's dust!"

With Rena safe in the shack, and Fargo down to one bullet, he decided not to roll the dice against such well-armed and skillful killers. Fargo realized now he had again underestimated them, but swore on the spot he wouldn't make that mistake again.

He waited until the sounds of scuffling feet faded, managing to feed three more beans into the wheel. Then he raced back out toward the flat bed of Death Valley, ears trained for any sound. A spur jingled in the darkness somewhere to his right, and Fargo swiveled toward the sound.

But the darkness was complete, and he spotted nothing. Moments later two horses shot off at a gallop as both men sank steel into their mounts.

"We didn't make too good a showing," Fargo admitted to Scotty.

"Them two are some in a fight—that's for sure," Scotty agreed. "But me 'n' you are still sassy, and they didn't get the Boston princess. Looks like we won."

Rena was nearly hysterical when they returned to the shack. "Skye! Scotty! Thank God you're all right!" she said in a welter of excitement.

"How 'bout you?" Fargo asked. "I heard a shot from in here."

She held up her derringer. "You saved me by ordering me to have this ready. I wounded him, but only slightly. Still, it was enough to rattle him so that when you shot at him, he let me go."

Fargo nodded. "All in all, we got lucky. But those buzzards will try again, and next time we better have more than luck on our side if we ever hope to leave this valley upright."

14

When the copper-tinted sun broke over the Funeral Mountains the next morning, Fargo was already on guard duty. In fact, he had decided they would be on watch day and night now, with Rena pitching in for daylight stints.

"I been thinking," Fargo told his two companions over a meager breakfast eaten outside before the sun heated up. "I don't much favor the idea of letting an enemy strike our digs without answering blow for blow. It builds their confidence that they can just play us like pianos."

"That rings right," Scotty agreed. "But poke not fire with a sword 'n' all that. Skye, Mad Dog and his redheaded sidekick might be spawn of the devil, but them boys could shoot the eye out of a buzzard at two hunnert yards. How do we get at 'em without gettin' our guts irrigated?"

"We'd need a diversion. But what we could really use is another can of blasting powder—got one?"

Scotty nodded. "I bought two in Virginia City before I left. Figured to use 'em here in Death Valley to mebbe expose a lode of color."

"Could I have it?" Fargo asked.

"Sure you can have it. Ain't worth a kiss-my-ass to me if I'm dead. What's your plan?"

"Depends," Fargo told him. "That diversion I mentioned—are you good for a frolic?"

Scotty puffed his unimpressive chest out. "Sure. I got snow on the roof, but my fires ain't banked yet. And I ain't seized up in the hinges yet, neither. What's on the spit?"

"Nothing fancy. They think they slapped us down good by digging up Matt Conway. They think we're weak in the knees now, so you're gonna lure those two reptiles out of their mine shaft, then I'm gonna sneak in and blow the place up."

Scotty shook with silent mirth. "Skye, that's slicker than snot on a saddle horn. 'Course, it might get us both killed. But I've yet to meet a man who's figured out how to cheat the Reaper."

Fargo grinned. "A man after my own heart."

Rena cleared her throat. Her sun hat had been ruined in her fall up in the mountains, but she had pulled a lacquered straw hat with a gay ostrich feather from her panniers.

"If you are both killed," she asked Fargo, "what about me?"

"Frankly," he replied, "you should have worried about your safety *before* you came to Death Valley. Now you'll have to take your chances."

Her face stretched into a petulant frown. "I suppose that's so. But do I have to stay here?"

"No," Fargo told her. "We don't know where those two are. They could attack here after me and Scotty ride out. You're gonna be hiding in a cabin."

Her ivory face paled to chalk. "Where the Conways were slaughtered? Skye, no! I could never—"

"Whack the cork," he snapped. "This is no time to get squeamish. The fat's in the fire. You won't be there long. It's safer than this place—Mad Dog doesn't want to go near it since murdering the family."

Fargo grabbed his tack from inside and moved around back, the other two following suit. "And Rena?" he added as he tossed the folded blanket onto the Ovaro. "Don't make any excursions to that cavern. If those two spot you, you're in for the worst hurt in the world."

He stepped into the stirrup and pushed up and over. "Now hold down the talk and pay attention to everything. Those two killers proved last night they aren't just dangerous— they're also smart."

Before leaving Rena at the cabin, all three horsebackers rode to the upper plateau of Grapevine Canyon and watered their mounts.

"I was half afraid that we'd find another Conway," Fargo admitted.

" 'Pears Mad Dog is more interested in fillin' graves than emptyin' 'em," Scotty suggested.

They rode back down toward the wide mouth of the canyon. Fargo ducked inside the cabin to make sure it was safe. Although not a superstitious man, the Trailsman felt his scalp tingle from the presence of the dead. It reminded him why the two remaining members of the Barton gang had to be killed no matter how long it took.

It required a bit of coaxing, but they got Rena's chestnut gelding inside the cabin and out of sight.

Fargo and Scotty then rode around to the western wall of the valley, staying in the shade close to the scree and boulders.

"I'm going to hole up in cover," Fargo explained, "while you ride past the mine right out in the open. But *don't* ride into easy rifle range. The entrance is hidden, so you'll have to shoot to get their attention. You're also going to shout something they'll be glad to hear. . . ."

Despite his nervous fear, Scotty laughed and slapped his thigh. "By God, I'll do it, Skye. But Christsakes, don't take too long settin' off that powder, huh? Won't take them two outlaws long to salt my tail."

Fargo rode as close to the mine as he dared, then reined off into the boulders, not far from where he'd killed Pepe Lopez. Scotty tugged the Remington from his belt and thumped General Washington with both heels, kicking him up to a gallop.

He fired at the bottomless blue sky. "Hey, you stinkin' sons of bitches!" his gravel-pan voice roared out. "Ain't neither of you got a tallywhacker on you! You kilt Skye Fargo last night, now come get *me*, you white-livered Aunt Nancys!"

Fargo held his breath in suspense, but not for long. Mad Dog and the redhead called Taffy bolted out onto the desert floor and gave chase to the prospector. Evidently, the welcome comment about killing Fargo had lowered their guards.

Fargo gigged his Ovaro forward, then reined off into the screening boulders in front of the mine and swung down, tossing the reins forward to hold his stallion. He dug the can of blasting powder from a saddle pocket and hurried inside.

Three horses, in various stages of neglect, were ground-reined near the entrance. Fargo liberated all three with sharp whacks on their rumps. A quick glance around the mine shaft told him where to detonate the powder. He opened the can and shook out a fuse line of black powder. The place was filled with supplies, probably stolen: boxes of ammunition (Fargo pocketed several), extra saddles, clothing and boots and U.S. Army rations. Fargo could have used more of it, but there was only time to destroy it.

He dug a lucifer from his shirt, thumb-scratched it to life, and touched off the fuse line. With the black powder fizzling and sparking, he ran toward the entrance.

About fifteen feet from the opening, the bottom fell out for Fargo.

A horse blanket lay spread open on the floor of the mine. By sheer accident Fargo had not stepped on it coming in, but his right foot plunged down onto it going out—and kept on plunging. The blanket covered a crude pitfall trap, obviously intended to give the outlaws extra security at night.

The bottom, Fargo saw in a heart-stopping glance, was far enough down to make climbing out difficult. But his trail-honed reflexes made him throw his arms out to both sides, checking his plummet. However, fast-forward momentum caused Fargo's forehead to slam against the front edge of the trap.

A bright-orange starburst exploded inside his skull, and Fargo fought with all his strength and will to resist blacking out. Behind him, the line of black powder burned rapidly, eating up valuable seconds. Fargo shook off the pain and dizziness, and flexed his arms mightily, lifting himself out of the pitfall with a harsh grunt. When he glanced over his shoulder, he felt his bowels go loose and heavy—the burning fuse was only inches from the tipped-over can!

Fargo completed the final fifteen feet to the entrance in a few strides and catapulted himself through the opening, tucking and rolling to the right just as the headframed entrance belched fire and smoke and a deadly load of rocks and ore tailings. The noise of explosion, in that confined space, made his ears ring and dulled his hearing.

He had left the Ovaro behind cover, and his trusty stallion did not desert him. Fargo vaulted into the saddle.

When he hit the open desert, he felt his blood singing. The two murderers had given up their pursuit of Scotty to rush back and salvage what they could from the burning mine.

Fargo speared his rifle from its scabbard in case they changed their minds. However, they were content with a few snap-shots at him, all whizzing wide. A grin divided his face as he joined Scotty and looped north toward Grapevine Canyon.

"Whoopie doodle!" Scotty shouted. "I ain't had so much fun since the hogs ate Uncle Pete!"

"You best enjoy it while you can," Fargo advised. "When those two yacks see how much they've lost, it'll put blood in their eyes. There *will* be a set-to."

Rena ran outside to meet them as they rode up to the cabin. "I heard the explosion from here," she told Skye. "Will it force them to give up?"

He swung down and threw the bridle so his pinto could drink from the barrel under the slope-off roof.

"Rena, you know damn well they can't give up," Fargo chided her. "It's root hog or die, and they know it."

Fargo didn't misinterpret the keen disappointment in her face. "You still want a crack at those jewels, don't you?" he asked. "Like I said, you won't be stealing them while I'm in charge, so push it out of your thoughts."

"Stuff!" she shot back. "It's not stealing now that it's been in the newspapers, it's . . . why, it's like salvage of gold doubloons on the high seas. If I don't find them, someone else will. At least I was . . . close to Winslowe."

Scotty snorted. "Aww, that's cowplop. You—"

"Never mind, both of you," Fargo cut in. "You're swattin' at gnats while tigers eat us alive. Don't think we're in the clear just because half the gang are dead. The most dangerous half is still alive."

Fargo pulled at his chin while he studied the cabin. "What's it like inside there?" he asked Rena.

She gave him a startled glance. "Why, if you can avoid looking at all the blood and gore downstairs, it's quite comfortable compared to our shack. There's even a full-length mirror."

"And much thicker walls," Fargo added. "And it sits in the open so it's hard to sneak up on."

"Are you thinkin' we should move in?" Scotty asked.

"Why not? The shack was fine until Mad Dog found out we were there. This place is easier to defend and safer from bullets. It's also a lot closer to Furnace Creek."

"I'm like the Injins," Scotty said. "I don't much cotton to stayin' where folks was kilt. The way the Conways died, their spirits is most likely hoverin' in pain close by. Still, all your reasons make sense, Skye."

"A spirit in pain," Rena assured him, "won't hurt mortals who are trying to help. Skye was Matt's friend. Besides, there's provisions in the cabin—jerked meat, coffee, sugar, even some air-tights of peaches and Gail Borden's condensed milk. Why waste them so we can gnaw on sardines?"

"Have you already heisted the jewels?" Scotty said sarcastically, but Fargo cut in quickly.

"I said knock it off, both of you. Let's make a quick trip to the shack for our gear and the grain we left there."

Fargo rode with his Henry across his thighs, but evidently Mad Dog and Taffy were still salvaging what they could from the mine. Fargo and his companions packed the few possessions in the shack and once again headed north toward the upper end of Death Valley, withering in afternoon heat that was at least 130 degrees.

"Rider ahead," Fargo announced, immediately pulling the field glasses from a saddle pocket.

A tall, skinny man in a slouch hat and new suit of black broadcloth was just entering the mouth of Grapevine Canyon on a big gray. Fargo studied his stubbled profile and saw a face more pious than criminal.

"Looks like a preacher headed for water," Scotty remarked.

"Does, don't it?" Fargo said from a deadpan. "Let's give him the hail. Right now I want no strangers in the canyon."

Fargo kicked the Ovaro from a trot to a canter, a grueling pace in this desert heat. When he was within hearing of the stranger, he sheathed his Henry and gave a shout. When the rider glanced behind him, Fargo raised one hand high in the universal sign that a man approached with no weapon drawn.

The horsebacker made no effort to escape, and when Fargo drew closer he saw a welcoming smile on the man's grimy, sunburned face. He had prominent throat muscles like taut cords.

"God bless you, brothers and sisters in the Lord!" he called out. "It's wonderful to see fellow human beings in this harsh land—the pressure of things invisible weighs on a man, and right now I'm pure people-starved. The name's Lemuel Jones."

Fargo, whose right hand stayed near his holster, greeted him cordially and introduced Scotty and Rena. "You appear to be a man of the cloth," Fargo added.

"That I am, Brother Fargo, that I am. I've left the Mormon colony of San Bernardino on my way to Virginia City to save souls on the Comstock."

Scotty guffawed. "No offense, Rev, but you'd have better luck walkin' on water. I just left Virginia City, and *them* boys won't take kindly to no soul-savin'. That place is Satan's flophouse on earth."

Jones gave a tolerant smile. "No man's labor is wasted in the Lord, Brother McDaniels. Besides, I'm not a hell-and-damnation preacher. My tools are smiles and kind words."

Those weren't his only tools, Fargo thought as he glanced at the preacher's long saddle boot.

"I see that's a Sharps Big Fifty you've brought along," Fargo remarked. "Fires fifty-caliber slugs that pack a whopping seven hundred grains of powder. Mighty vindictive weapon for a man of smiles and kind words."

"Skye," Rena objected, embarrassed by this treatment of a cleric. "Any man traveling in the West has a right to defend himself."

"And hunt, Sister Collins," the preacher added. "Brother Fargo is right, this *is* a powerful weapon. But I'm a terrible shot, and the Sharps allows even a poor marksman to bring down game."

"Makes sense," Fargo agreed. But he also eyed the hand-tooled holster with its Smith and Wesson six-shooter—walnut grips just like his own Colt. Why would a self-proclaimed preacher and "terrible shot" file off the notch sight? The only reason Fargo knew of was to prevent the gun from snagging when it was jerked from the holster.

Fargo had spent time around Mormons, and he had never known this clannish group to use the words "brother" and "sister" with Gentiles, as they called anyone outside the Mormon religion.

Casually, he asked the supposed holy man, "Say, how does Prophet Joseph Smith like life in Salt Lake City?"

"Takes to it like a duck to water, Brother Fargo. It's God's land wherever you find a Mormon church."

Fargo's Colt leaped into his hand.

Rena gasped. "Skye! What in the world?"

"Joseph Smith," Fargo said, steely blue eyes piercing the phony like a pair of bullets, "died years ago east of the Mississippi. And Mormons worship in meeting houses, not churches. This jasper is no more a Mormon than my horse."

"Shit take it!" Scotty burst out. "You didn't slicker me, neither, mister," he blustered. "I'm smarter than you look, and you don't size up like no preacher."

"How did you know, Skye?" Rena asked.

"When you travel as much as I have," Fargo replied, "you develop a sense for impostors. Right from the start, something about this jasper just didn't tally."

"Look," Jones said mildly, "if I've overstepped—"

"Your mouth runs like a whippoorwill's ass, *preacher*," Fargo cut him off. "Now skin that bean shooter out *slow* and drop it. If that muzzle comes up even for an eyeblink, I'll burn you where you sit."

The man did as ordered. "Brother Fargo, may I be eternally damned if I'm lying. You see—"

"Bottle it." Everything in Fargo's face smiled except his eyes. "Scotty, Rena, ride on up to the cabin. Take your horses inside."

"But . . . where will you be?" Rena demanded.

"Extracting some information from our friend," Fargo replied. "Now break dust."

"All right, Mr. Fargo," the man said after the other two rode off, "I confess I'm a fake preacher. But there's no need to bust a vein over it. I'm a sneak thief and the preacher act makes it easier to steal."

Fargo's shoulder muscles corded like bunched lariats when he grabbed Jones and ripped him from the saddle. The man fell in an ungainly heap on the salt-rock desert floor.

"You're a goddamn liar," Fargo told him in a caustic tone, thumb-cocking his Colt. "You're the fifth member of

Mad Dog Barton's gang. Your front name's Fenton and you just got out of jail in Los Angeles."

"Fargo, that's spun truck! I—"

The Colt bucked, and the grifter screamed in agony when the bullet punched through the toe of his right boot. Fargo cocked again. "Fess up, cockroach, or the left foots gets one too."

"No, please, for Christ sakes! It's true, I'm Fenton Kinney!"

Fargo nodded, his face filled with grim purpose. He threw the reins forward and dismounted. He picked up the Smith and Wesson and slid it back in Kinney's holster.

"Stand up," Fargo ordered. "That wounded foot will hold your weight."

"Wh-why?"

"I didn't start this fight in the valley," Fargo replied, leathering his short gun. "But I mean to finish it. And there's no way in hell I'm letting you join your pals so you can help kill us."

Kinney pushed awkwardly to his feet. "You mean . . . you're forcing me into a showdown?"

"It's more of a chance than you'd ever give me," Fargo replied. "Now quit jackin' your jaws and skin it back."

"Fargo, damn it, this ain't—"

"Skin it, Kinney, you yellow cur."

"Fargo, my gun ain't even loaded. It's—"

With impressive speed Kinney shucked out his six-gun, but Fargo was quicker. He drilled the owlhoot straight through the pump and watched his body collapse like an empty sack. He stripped the man and his horse of all ammo and feed plus the Smith and Wesson and the Sharps Big Fifty. Knowing the horse would instinctively seek water beyond the desert, Fargo stripped the gray of tack and slapped his rump, sending him up the canyon.

Fargo slanted a glance toward the body on the ground. Though he took no pleasure in the kill, neither did he feel remorse. This man was here to commit red-handed murder, whereas Fargo had at least given him a fighting chance.

"Rot in hell, preacher," Fargo said aloud, and then he tied off the big Sharps before stepping into leather and heading up the canyon.

15

Toward nightfall Mad Dog Barton called out sharply, "Up ahead, Taffy! *Damn!* Looks like Fenton locked horns with Fargo."

Both riders were approaching the broad mouth of Grapevine Canyon, which formed a long slope upward toward the north. They swung down and held their reins as they squatted over the body of Fenton Kinney. Taffy rolled it over.

"One shot through the heart," Mad Dog announced, adding a string of curses. The flat yellow disks of his eyes seemed to glow with malevolence. "Skye Fargo don't waste a bullet, does he?"

"Didn't waste any time when he blew up the Busted Flat, neither," Taffy said. "We lost a damned good hideout, not to mention that chamois pouch with all them stock coupons we stole in El Paso. Damn near three thousand dollars."

Both men's faces were brassy and hostile in the fading sunlight.

"Fenton wasn't born in the woods to be scared by an owl," Mad Dog said, staring at the dead man's bluish face and staring eyes. "He could fool any man with his preacher act, even real preachers. If Fargo twigged his game that quick, he *must* be a dangerous man."

Taffy gave that a harsh bark of scorn. "You ain't figured that out till right now? Ask the Kid and Pepe if he's dangerous."

Taffy looked up from Fenton to stare at his boss. "This makes three of us he's killed, Mad Dog. This Trailsman is everything he's cracked up to be."

"And we ain't? I always said Fargo is a mighty conse-

117

quential man. But, pard, we damn near doused his light when we attacked the shack last night. That old man with him is worthless as tits on a boar hog—if we can put Fargo in front of a bullet, that sketchin' bitch is *ours*, and so are them hidden sparklers that was writ about in the newspaper."

Mad Dog adjusted the revolvers in his sash until they pointed butts-first again, the quickest draw he'd ever found.

"That sketchin' bitch," he repeated, lust thickening his voice. "We ever get our hands on her, I'll be gettin' my second poke before she catches her breath from the first. That little cottontail could make a dead man hard."

Taffy nodded. "Straight arrow. And that damn Fargo's prob'ly gettin' it whenever he's hungry."

Both men searched the body and stood up.

"Looks like Fargo got the Sharps," Mad Dog said. "Unless Fenton's horse bolted with it."

"That gun scores kills out to a mile," Taffy fretted. "How we gonna do this without Fenton, Mad Dog?"

Mad Dog's lips eased back to reveal narrow teeth like fangs. "How? Kill it, gut it, skin it, run a spit through it, cook it. That's how."

"This is Skye Fargo, not a rabbit," Taffy snapped.

"Don't get your bowels in an uproar, Welshman," Mad Dog said. "Look, earlier we seen him water their horses and go back to the Conway cabin. They ain't left yet, right?"

"Looks that way."

"Which means they moved from the shack along the east wall of the valley to the Conway cabin. So we'll take the shack they deserted. More important—you know how any wood in Death Valley is soon sapped dry."

"That cabin is a tinderbox," Taffy said, catching on. "You're thinkin' we should burn them out?"

"Why the hell not? Even if they get out alive, we can hide in the boulders and pick them off like nits from a hound. We'll have flames to guide our aim in the dark."

Taffy stubbornly shook his head. "You seen how Fargo likes to post sentries. There's open ground all around that cabin. He'll pick *us* off like nits."

"Sure," Mad Dog countered, "if we're stupid enough to

cross that ground ourselves. But just a whoop and a holler from here we got everything we need."

Taffy followed the direction of Mad Dog's eyes. "Sure, the Scorpion's Lair."

"Now you're whistling. We was just up there, and we seen a hay wagon loaded with bales. Who's gonna stop us from taking it? We already killed the owner of that roach pit, and that hell hag sister of his damn near give us a medal for doing it."

Taffy was rapidly warming to the idea. "Hell yes! Their only customers are lost pilgrims and desert rats who prospect for gold. They don't like shootin' scrapes."

Mad Dog grunted. "The beauty of it is, there's already a reg'lar wagon track that goes right down to the cabin from the lip of the canyon near the Lair. Once we get that hay wagon locked in them ruts, and fire it, it'll roll smack-bang into the cabin with a good push."

"Sure. And we won't even need a team to get it in place—that old dobbin they keep up at the Lair can pull it downslope while we ride the brake."

"We chock the wheels soon as we're in place," Mad Dog said. "The slope'll take it quick, once we tie the tongue up and pull the chocks. We'll wait until after midnight."

"Likely be a sentry," Taffy cautioned. "Maybe even Fargo."

"Yeah, but until we actually fire the hay, which won't take no time at all the way the wind whips at night, he won't know we're out there. And they ain't likely to have enough water to douse the fire. They'll *have* to come outside, and we'll be in darkness while that fire puts them in daylight. Just remember: We don't want to kill the woman, just grab her."

"Kill her? Would you toss away a juicy steak?" Taffy quipped. "But it's Fargo we need to worry about. That bastard has planted three of our gang, and he just blew up one of our best hideouts. Unless we kill him, the whole plan caves in—right on us."

Fargo gazed out the kitchen window of the Conway cabin, watching Grapevine Canyon shift colors in the fading sunlight.

"See anything, Skye?" Rena asked nervously. She carried the "preacher's" six-gun constantly now.

Fargo shook his head. "With only two of them left, they won't likely try a daylight attack. I'll start outside sentry duty soon as it's dark."

Rena paced the small room. "My goodness, I'm so nervous I'm perspiring."

"Be glad of it," Fargo remarked absently. "In the desert, when you stop sweating you're in trouble."

"God, *why* did I ever come to Death Valley?" Rena lamented. "The jewels aren't worth it. I see that now."

"Strike a light," Fargo barbed. "Illumination at last."

"I shoulda hauled my freight outta here, too," Scotty told Rena. "But it ain't just me and you, and it ain't just this valley. There's people all over the frontier who got no good reason for being here."

"Both you calamity howlers," Fargo cut in, "need to let it alone. And stop carving your own tombstones. I intend to win this fight and to get all of us out of here alive."

"We could sneak out this very night," Rena suggested. "And report the murder of the Conways to the first law we meet."

Fargo, shifting his Henry to his right hand, shook his head. "Nix on that. Mad Dog and the redhead will just slip away, too. Besides, they've tried to put sunlight through me, too, and I don't let any man just walk away from that."

Outside, the desolate wind that constantly scoured Death Valley made a ghostly sound between a howl and a shriek. Hearing it, Fargo felt sad all of a sudden. He missed rivers and creeks, grass and trees, the dawn chorus of birds. The mountains here were sterile, the sun murderous, the valley bed a salt-encrusted slab of hard bedrock that strained a horse's knees and a man's tailbone. But Fargo had buried the three people who were murdered in this cabin, and he was going nowhere until he curled Barton's and the redhead's toes.

"Full moon tonight," Fargo said. "The hardcases know we're here by now, but we'll skip lighting any lanterns. There's three beds up in the loft, so we'll all sleep there."

"I'm a bunch-quitter," Scotty grumped. "Ain't my way to live in homes with people."

"All right, sleep in the next room with the animals. *They* won't mind your smell."

Fargo set his Henry atop the old Franklin stove and drew his Colt in the fading light, spinning the cylinder to check his loads. "I'm going out to take the first guard. Scotty, I'll roust you out later."

After carefully studying the terrain, Fargo slipped outside into the evening darkness. The vicious wind, whipped to a fury by its long journey up the narrow and empty valley, almost grabbed his hat. Fargo pressed it down and slanted the brim to protect his eyes.

He walked an ever-changing route during those first hours of darkness, ears and eyes trained up the canyon and down. Except for the wind, which was especially loud among the thousands of boulders littering Grapevine Canyon, Fargo heard nothing ominous. He forced himself to a long stint.

When the yellowish tinge of the moon told him it was almost midnight, he went back inside and climbed a short ladder into the loft, shaking Scotty awake. Fargo slanted a gaze toward Rena's bed but resisted the urge—she appeared to be sound asleep, and Fargo's eyelids were so heavy they felt weighted with coins.

"Skye?" her sleepy voice called to him after Scotty climbed down.

"Yeah?"

"All I have on is my chemise. Why don't you climb in with me?"

Fargo could rarely say no to a willing female. He leaned down to tug off his boots when Scotty's voice, rigid with fright, pulled him up short.

"Skye! Get out here, boy! By the Lord Harry, we got bad trouble!"

Fargo saw the trouble the moment he ducked to the only upstairs window that faced north. A mass of bright orange flames was hurtling down the slope straight for the cabin, following the deep grooves of an old wagon track he'd noticed earlier.

"Throw on some clothes," he barked at Rena as he headed for the ladder. "Then grab that six-shooter and take cover downstairs. But don't go near any windows."

Fargo didn't bother with the rungs, simply dropping to the first floor and bending his knees slightly for the landing. The moment he hit the floor, there was a loud crash out front as the burning conveyance rammed the cabin. Gunshots opened up, the solid crack of rifles firing high-power bullets. Fargo dove through a window and saw with dismay that a wagon loaded with burning hay was lighting up the night. Constant wind fueled the ravenous flames.

Scotty, game as always, had covered down behind a boulder near a front corner of the cabin. But relentless gunfire kept him trapped there. Unable to get a bead on the shooters, Scotty wisely conserved his ammo.

Fargo, however, had spotted muzzle fire on a northwest line farther up the canyon.

"Scotty!" he shouted. "The cabin's about to ignite! Without showing yourself, raise your gun over that boulder and shoot just to your left. Three bursts, two shots each. We need to distract them so I can clear that wagon."

At first Fargo's hasty plan worked. Scotty's return fire drew the attention of Mad Dog Barton and Taffy, and Fargo was able to hurry over to the portable inferno and set his back against the wagon. Before he could even make his first effort to push it back, however, the intense flames clearly showed his enemies where he was.

Quick as a finger snap the shooters switched targets, and Fargo was caught in a hellish swarm of deadly lead.

The wind-rip from several bullets feather-tickled his skin and forced him to lie flat to avoid sure death. Between fire and gunfire he was caught in the deadliest pincers trap on the frontier. Cursing, he rolled away from the burning wagon. That made him less of a target, but also left hot, snapping flames to lick greedily at the cabin—flames fanned by the natural bellows of the gusty wind.

Fargo rolled into semidark shadows and tossed the Henry into his shoulder, estimating the yardage of the muzzle fire above. Working the Henry's lever like a pump handle, he sprayed sixteen shots at the hidden killers. For the moment he'd forced them to cover, and the rain of lead abated.

"Skye!" Rena's hysterical voice shouted from inside. "The cabin's on fire! Smoke is pouring in, and my horse and Scotty's mule are terrified!"

Fargo was racing back toward the burning wagon again.

He could hear the mounts braying and neighing in fright although the battle-hardened Ovaro was still quiet.

"You're all right for now!" he called back. "Flames won't get you this soon. If breathing gets hard, go to the floor or break a window. The hobbles will restrain your horse and General Washington."

When he saw the cabin, however, Fargo felt his stomach go queasy. The unstripped logs had started to burn and would soon be engulfed. He was able to brace himself against the wagon and push it a few feet away, suffering singed hair and a few burns, before the lethal rifle fire again started pouring in.

Bullets chunked all around him, and Fargo cursed as he was again forced to lie prone.

"Rena!" he called, keeping his voice as low as he could.

"Yes?"

"That rifle I took from the phony preacher—it's leaning against the wall near the door. Open the door and slide it out. And the chamois pouch with the bullets for it."

Even as Fargo spoke, deadly 500-grain bullets tossed grit in his eyes and struck within inches of killing him. The moment he heard the door close, he leaped up, grabbed the Sharps and the pouch of .50-caliber bullets, and raced back into the shadows. The twelve-pound Big Fifty felt reassuring in his hands.

"You boys like big bullets with plenty of powder load?" he muttered as he sprawled again. "Meet the king of the smoke poles."

The single-shot Sharps was already loaded. Fargo raised the sights, added a few clicks on the windage knob, and drew a bead on the muzzle blast above him. The powerful gun actually moved him backward when it mule-kicked into his shoulder, the sound deep and potent as the 700-grain load exploded with deadly authority.

Fargo didn't let up. As quickly as he could work the bolt and roll open the breechblock, he inserted a new shell and fired. The return fire from above ceased altogether as the intimidating "hand cannon" forced the two nervous murderers to safer cover.

"Scotty!" Fargo called out. "I don't know if they've retreated or just taken cover, so move fast! Run inside the cabin and grab the water bag."

Fargo hustled back to the cabin. The wagon, which he'd moved away from the structure, was finally burning itself out. But the cabin was burning in several places and on the verge of widespread engulfment. The muscles in his arms, shoulders, and back steeling with the effort, Fargo picked up the wooden water barrel and emptied it on the worst spot.

Scotty came outside lugging the gutbag. Fargo untied the rawhide whang holding it shut and began sloshing water on the flames. By the time he'd finished, he and Scotty were able to extinguish the rest of the blaze with a water-soaked blanket.

Fargo poked his head inside. "Rena, how the animals doing?"

"Calming down," her musical voice called back. "Your stallion hardly seemed to notice."

"He's a warhorse," Fargo said proudly.

Fargo shut the door and looked at Scotty. "They could've fired at us some more by now," he remarked. "That Big Fifty must have sent them back out of range. Now the fire's out, and most likely they figure it's too much risk to nab Rena."

"It was a good strike, though," Scotty said. "Hadn't been for your cojones, this cabin would be embers, and then we'd be in a world of hurt with them tossin' lead down on us."

Fargo nodded. "It was well planned. These two have crafty criminal minds and plenty of experience. Which means we can't let them keep hatching schemes. One of them is bound to work."

"How in Sam Hill do we stop them?" Scotty demanded.

"Best way I know of," Fargo replied, "is to kill them before they kill us. Which means we quit hunkering down. We take the fight to them, the sooner the better."

16

We take the fight to them, the sooner the better.

Brave words, Fargo told himself the next morning, and true words, too. It was dangerous to let an enemy define the terms of a battle, but how could he stop them when he didn't even know where they were staying now—nor did they have a woman to protect as he did.

"Dadgumit!" Scotty fumed as he stoked the old Franklin stove with firewood Matt Conway had hauled in from the east slope of the Sierras. He wore canvas trousers stained with ore and a shirt sewn from sacking. "Mad Dog and his pard can pretty much call the shots right now, the double-poxed hounds."

Fargo was busy making a quick check of the fire damage. "It's a hell-buster," he admitted. "Anybody with a good plan can toss it into the hotchpot."

"You know my plan," Rena said, climbing down from the loft. "We find the jewels and leave."

"And just let two of the worst killers in the Barton gang off the hook?" Fargo asked. "No, thanks. They murdered five people right in front of you—that *ought* to matter."

"It does," she retorted. "But I saw two hundred die in a steamboat explosion on the Potomac, too. The dead are still dead, so why shouldn't we get rich?"

"Them ain't even your sparklers," Scotty reminded her from the kitchen. "Just 'cause you diddled this Winslowe fellow don't make you family."

Fargo cut the argument short. "The jewels stay right where they are. And, Rena, Matt was my friend. We trailed together for a winter. If you want to strike out on your own, I can't stop you. But John Barton is one mad dog

125

who requires a muzzle and a short leash, and I mean to trap him."

Rena pouted but Fargo ignored her, amazed at how little fire damage had affected the inside of the cabin. The drapes, made of heavy monk's cloth to block the sun, were slightly singed, as was a needlework footstool, and a pane of glass had melted. Otherwise, Fargo's efforts had paid off.

"Grub pile!" Scotty called from the kitchen.

"Let's fix our plates and take 'em outside," Fargo suggested. "It's easier to stand watch."

Thanks to the Conway larder, they enjoyed a breakfast of flapjacks and honey. Outside, in the ringing heat, not even the dusty twang of grasshoppers' wings hinted at any life in Death Valley.

Scotty pointed down the canyon where it opened onto the valley. "When you're traveling from east to west, the deserts develop gradual like. But, mister, once you leave that forest coast of the Pacific and turn east, everything changes quicker than an Injin goin' to crap."

Fargo nodded. To get here he had ridden up into a pass over the Sierra Nevadas. A few miles later, everything before him was barren desert. The Sierras were the rain barrier that made this area.

Rena was cleaning her teeth with a hog-bristle brush. She pulled it from her mouth. "Just because we're in the desert, does that mean we can't have a bath? *All* of us need one."

She pointed toward a wooden bathtub sitting upside down by the cabin door. "The water hole is right above us. Just a couple trips with that big water bag of yours would fill the tub."

Fargo thought about it. It was common, in that day, for several bathers to take turns in one tub of water. Besides, they *were* smelling a little ripe.

"Scotty, roll that tub inside the cabin," Fargo said. "Leave it right inside the door. No reason we can't have a bath long as we keep an eye out for trouble. Gives me a chance to water our mounts."

Fargo poured the remaining water from the gutbag into the tub. He had already brought the horses and mule, suffering from cooped-up fever, outside and hobbled them

126

under the slope-off roof. He tacked the Ovaro and tied the gutbag to his saddle.

"Stay outside," he ordered Scotty, "with your gun to hand. I can see the cabin from the upper plateau, but at the first sign of trouble bust a cap to signal me. And don't forget—the Sharps is loaded and standing just inside the door. Shoot from a prone position, and don't be afraid to blow a horse out from under its rider."

Rena raised the Smith and Wesson they'd taken from the phony preacher. "I have seven shots counting my derringer. We'll be all right."

Fargo made one trip with all the mounts, leading the mule and the chestnut by their bridle reins. He filled the gutbag, then let all three mounts tank up. He had guessed that just one bag would fill the rest of the tub, and it did.

"You go first," he told Rena. "Then Scotty and me. We'll be on guard outside."

"Leave the door open, please," she told him. "That Mad Dog is a clever monster, and I want you able to see me at all times."

Scotty snorted at this but said nothing. He went around to the side of the cabin that faced the mouth of the canyon. Fargo glanced at the sun on the floor of the cabin and knew it was midmorning—about the time that lazy outlaws might be stirring. He grabbed the heavy Sharps and hauled it outside.

Rena didn't even pretend at modesty. She peeled out of her clothing under Fargo's appreciative eye and stuck one exploratory foot in the water.

"Warm but not hot," she called out the door to him. "Just right."

The heavy but high-riding breasts showed above the edge of the tub as she sudsed them and rinsed, enjoying Fargo's attention.

Fargo remembered to keep close watch on the surrounding terrain, too.

"Skye?" Rena called outside to him.

"Yeah?"

"No offense, but you don't seem the type to have dealt with large sums of money. Do you realize the true value of those jewels?"

"Don't really care."

"Well, I do," she insisted. "Back east I get sick of truckling to people of rank. If I had those jewels, I could tell them to kiss my you-know-what."

"I'm no lawyer," Fargo replied, "but I've heard them blow. Seems like you're getting lost property mixed up with abandoned property. Those jewels still belong to the Winslowe family."

"You care about such distinctions?" she demanded.

"You'd care, too, if they were your jewels."

"You're hopeless," she accused, a series of angry splashes ending the conversation.

She toweled off, dressed, and called Scotty in for his turn.

"I need to make a necessary trip," she told Fargo when she stepped outside.

A batboard jakes stood well beyond the cabin, tucked among surrounding boulders.

"Hold on until I take a look," he told her, walking all around the area. He moved back up toward the cabin. "Looks all right. Go ahead."

She grinned at him. "I'm glad you didn't take any longer—nature calls."

Rena headed upslope toward the jakes while Fargo listened to Scotty bellow out verses of "Lu-lu Girl" as he bathed within the house. Fargo heard the outhouse door meow open, then Rena's shrill scream rent the air. Despite the oven heat, Fargo felt his skin grain with alarm. He had checked all around the jakes, but never thought to check *inside*.

It might be a rattlesnake, Fargo told himself as he spun around on his heel, grounding both rifles and bringing his Colt up to the ready. But the only snake that shoved out of the jakes, using Rena as his protective shield, was Mad Dog Barton.

"Just can't cut the bacon lately, huh, Fargo?" Barton roweled him. "First we damn near burn you out, now I grab your whore in the shitter."

For a few moments, as Barton stared at Rena, he reminded Fargo of a winter bear—one who had just broken his sleep to eat and was voraciously hungry. Fargo automatically turned sideways to diminish Mad Dog's target. Scotty, blissfully ignorant of the sudden danger outside, still belted out bawdy songs inside the house.

"I might not cut bacon too good," Fargo replied, "but I carved up your Mexican just enough, and shot two white men to death besides. And counting you, there's two more I'll soon send to glory."

Mad Dog was clearly scared of the Trailsman and kept himself well covered by Rena, especially his head. "That he-bear talk don't cut no ice with me, crusader. Now, why'n'cha holster that thumb-buster before this little filly pulls up lame?"

Fargo knew that a scared man was more likely to be trigger-happy, and Mad Dog was sure acting fearful. Fargo also knew why Barton hadn't shot at him by now—the distance, about forty yards, was beyond the sure range of most draw-shoot killers. *But where's the redhead?* Fargo wondered desperately.

"You ain't hurting the girl," Fargo said bluntly. "You'll kill her eventually because her testimony will leave you dancing on air. But right now you need her to take you to those jewels."

Mad Dog had guessed by now that Fargo had overheard them in the mine talking about the Winslowe jewels—after all, that must have been how Fargo learned about Fenton coming.

"That won't spend, Fargo," he retorted. "Drop that artillery, or maybe I'll just check this little piece for a tit gun—"

The talk was all a distraction. Mad Dog suddenly sneaked a shot at Fargo. The bullet hummed wide, but Mad Dog left his right arm briefly exposed. Fargo snapped off a round, and blood fountained from Barton's forearm.

Mad Dog recovered instantly and filled his left hand, putting the six-gun's muzzle to Rena's ear. At the same time a rifle spoke its piece from the boulders above them, and a chunk flew out of the cabin's stick-and-mud chimney. Then a hidden horse sped into motion and Fargo spun his Colt into the holster, trading it for his Henry.

"Sure, you got a rifle!" Mad Dog shouted, blood spattering his white sailcloth trousers. "But all you can hit is my arms and legs. Hit me one more time, Fargo, and her brains will end up on the rocks."

Fargo had planned to bring the fight to them, but they were bringing it to him instead. Taffy, armed with a big repeating rifle, joined his comrade. Both men covering him from hard eyes, they led Rena toward hidden horses.

The shots had finally slapped Scotty back to the present. He threw a towel around himself and stepped out into the frying-pan heat.

"Skye!" Rena begged. "Take that shot anyway! The odds are better for me now than later!"

Fargo disagreed. He knew Mad Dog had no future if Rena lived and he would kill her now if forced to it. Fargo would rather try his luck later. He ignored Rena, almost out of sight now as her abductors moved her toward the horses.

"She's got a hard row to hoe now," Scotty said. "They'll rape the spirit out of her before they kill her."

"Not if we hit fast," Fargo said.

"Fast? Criminy, boy! We have to find 'em first."

Fargo crawled up onto one of the taller boulders and watched through his spyglasses. Nearly twenty minutes later he slid down.

"Don't worry, Scotty," he told the prospector. "We won't need to traipse all over hell finding them. They've headed right toward the shack we gave up."

Mad Dog had recently managed to steal an army medical kit from a log-cutting detail on the Humboldt River. He pulled bandages from it now, cursing the fiery stabs of pain in his arm. Rena sat alone near a window and dreaded what would come next.

Taffy helped him wrap a bandage. "Look, Mad Dog, time is pushing—for them as ain't been killed yet, which is me and you. We can get the jewels and we can kill the girl, but unless we kill Fargo, too, we're earmarked. And you shootin' that grog shop owner right in front of witnesses wasn't too smart. Neither is leaving that prospector alive."

Taffy turned his thin, sharp-nosed face toward Rena. The evident lust in his face made her skin crawl.

"Don't fret it," Barton told his friend. "Killing the bar dog was nothing—it won't get reported."

"Maybe not, but every day we tarry here is another chance we get linked to the Conways. It's no mystery he delivered your brother Lanny to the hangman."

Mad Dog hissed when Taffy wrapped the wound too tight. "Damn Fargo to hell! Taffy, before we leave we have to kill him. Was Fenton alive now, he'd come up with a good plan."

This time it was Mad Dog who stared at Rena, wind-cracked lips bloody and scabbed. His strange yellow eyes made him appear rabid.

"Hand me that cheerwater, Taffy," he said, nodding toward a bottle of bourbon on the table. "And build me a smoke."

The medical kit included a sharp lancet for boils and other surgery. Mad Dog pulled it out with his left hand.

"We ain't got much time, sketchin' bitch," Mad Dog warned her. "I'm givin' it to you with the bark still on it: When I got this arm fixed, you're takin' us to them jewels. Won't be no parlor tricks, neither, or they'll hear your screams in China."

Rena swallowed the hard stone in her throat. "I already know you're going to murder me for witnessing the Conway massacre. So what good are threats about the jewels?"

Mad Dog showed her the sharp-tipped lancet again, his face hard as carved granite. "There's quick death from a bullet to the head, and there's slow, screaming death while your skin and muscle are peeled back. You think on that."

Mad Dog devoured her with his eyes, still wincing as Taffy finished his arm. "Soon as this arm quits hurtin' like fire, I'm *takin'* you, girl. Right here in front of God and everybody."

He turned to Taffy again. "Don't matter how you slice it, if I had my druthers I'd avoid Fargo like the mouth of hell. But thanks to this blond bitch, we got him on us like ugly on a buzzard."

"There," Taffy said, finishing up. "If that wound don't mortify, you'll live."

"It makes me ireful!" Mad Dog shouted, making Rena flinch when he struck the trestle table with his good hand. "Ain't a one of us in the gang that Fargo hasn't killed or wounded."

Taffy's stomach growled loudly. "Damn this jerky and dried fruit. I wish we was dippin' soda biscuits into pot liquor."

"Never mind, muttonhead," Mad Dog snapped. "I'm

131

talkin' 'bout Fargo and how he's a one-man army. You know, twice he's used blasting powder against us, and now he's got Fenton's Big Fifty. Maybe we need to improve our arsenal."

"Too late now," Taffy replied. "We're stuck with what we have."

Rena watched Barton shake his head in disgust. "Like hell we are. You don't remember the Grubstake Mine down near Last Chance Valley? Maybe three years back?"

Taffy looked baffled for a few heartbeats, then suddenly snapped his fingers. "Oh, *hell* yes! Place went bust when the ore played out. We broke into the powder magazine and got us some dynamite."

"Well, then, that answers you the question of a better arsenal."

"You're gettin' ahead of the roundup," Taffy objected. "We cached that stuff by burying it here in the valley. Three years buried, and you're thinkin' it would still pack a kick?"

"Good chance," Mad Dog insisted. "I wrapped it all real good in a sheet of wagon canvas, and I doubt any rain has seeped down to it. It's only about a three-hour ride from here. Before we do another damn thing, let's go check that cache. With luck, we can blow Fargo and that old limp dick sky-high before they even miss us."

As one, the two men remembered Rena and stared over at her.

"You know it all now, don'tcha, sketchin' bitch?" Mad Dog snarled. "But there ain't one damn thing you can do about it. Matter fact, we're gonna give you the thrill of seein' your buckskin stud blasted to paste."

Mad Dog's left hand plucked a fancy revolver from his sash. "Now shuck off them clothes, sugar britches, and let's see what you got."

17

Fargo seemed in no immediate hurry to ride south toward the old shack. Scotty watched him move the Ovaro and General Washington to better shade. Though the day was still barely past forenoon, the July sun was a scorcher.

"The hell we waitin' on?" Scotty demanded. "A posse from heaven? We know where they are."

"Simmer down," Fargo told him. "We can't just go dundering in there without a plan. That shack is too well protected, especially since Rena sent half a mountain down on us. Mad Dog and Taffy are both dead shots, and besides, if we try to rush them, they'll kill Rena."

"Them two're smart," Scotty admitted. "That shithouse trick proves it. Even if Rena hadn't opened that door, it woulda been me or you, and Mad Dog woulda stitched us full of snake holes."

Fargo nodded. "I should've sent a few bullets into it to make sure, but I didn't think much about it. I never use the damn things if I can avoid 'em. I bollixed that one."

"It's did now. How many times have you pulled that gal's corset out of the fire? She started all this by coming out to a dangersome place where she shouldn't oughta be."

"I can't gainsay all that," Fargo said. "But this time it wasn't her fault, and we'll have to pull her corset out once more."

"So you got a plan?"

"It's scratched out in the dirt," Fargo said. "Nothing too fancy. But with you siding me, we'll make it work."

Scotty looked surprised. "You got that much faith in me?"

"Why shouldn't I? You're a mite scratchy when you're sober, but you're also dependable."

Scotty puffed out his chest. "Let's hear this plan."

"Not much to it. Since that rockslide, the shack is surrounded by more boulders than ever. You're gonna be on the north side with the Sharps and my Henry. I'm gonna be on the south side. Once I locate Rena, I'll signal to you where she is in the shack. Then you're going to blast a hole in the door with the Sharps and follow up with my Henry. While all this is going on, I'll get Rena's attention and toss a looped rope to her through one of the windows. Then, with you still filling that shack with lead, I'll haul her up to the boulders with me."

Scotty shook his head, not too impressed. "Good chance they'll kill her *and* you," he opined.

"Good chance," Fargo agreed. "But they'll kill her anyway. The best chance to spring her is right about now, when it's long enough for their battle fever to cool but too soon to expect us."

Scotty still didn't look too impressed. "That's your plan?"

"I've scratched out worse."

"Well, I guess every family tree has got its nuts."

Fargo grinned. "Oh, there's more. We can't shoot them out of that shack, but after you get out of the way I'm going to start another rockslide. With luck, we'll either smash the shack with them in it or drive them out into our sights."

"That part could work," Scotty agreed. "When do we leave?"

"All our weapons are ready, so I say right now."

Fargo slid the Sharps Big Fifty into the boot on Scotty's saddle. "Just one shot to get 'em nerve-jangled," he explained. "That weapon would unstring any man's nerves. But it's single-shot, so switch to the Henry immediately. I'll give it to you when we hide our mounts."

Both men hit leather and started down toward the mouth of the canyon.

Scotty cleared his throat. "You know, that Rena's got a tart mouth on her, and she's sneaky as a raccoon in the pantry. But she's got spunk, too. Them two could be rapin' her right now."

"They won't miss the chance," Fargo agreed. "But Mad

Dog is the ramrod, and he'll want first dibs. That wounded arm will have to be tended to first. We might be in time."

Scotty glanced around at the sterile and parched surroundings. He tried to spit in disgust, but his mouth was too dry. "I'm quits with this damn valley, Skye, happens I ever get out alive. Think I'll try the Front Range of the Rockies next."

"I won't lie to you," Fargo replied. "Bad as it is out here in Death Valley, I hate the big cities with their rules and laws more. Cities are even more dangerous than here, yet a man's not even free."

"You struck a lode there," Scotty admitted. "But there ain't nothin' here. 'Cept killers."

"Old man, this place still has its points. You never have to worry about the first hatch of mosquitoes dealing you misery every spring, or finding a horse ford over rivers. Rarely do you meet a hostile Indian and never a bear."

"Never a thirst parlor, neither," Scotty tossed in. "That damned Scorpion's Lair sells cheap Indian burner. I only like reg'lar brands. I miss creeks with crawdads in 'em, too, and tallgrass flowers."

Fargo surrendered with a laugh. "You win, Scotty. I'd guess it's close to a hundred twenty degrees right now and it's not even noon yet. Most places, my stallion can hold a canter almost all day and still conserve his wind and limbs. But in this salt-desert inferno, even a slow trot saps him."

By now the two riders had covered about half the distance to the hidden shack. Fargo ordered single file now as they reined in even closer to the piles of debris forming aprons at the base of the mountains.

"They've had time to fix Mad Dog's arm," Scotty remarked, his face grim. "Which means them two might be pressing their . . . attentions on Rena by now."

Fargo nodded. "We'll do what we can for her. But don't forget, we can't help her if we're dead. Just stay frosty, shoot plumb, and hope Rena is as smart as we think she is. If we don't pluck her out of that shack in the next half hour or so, she's most likely headed beyond the mountains—for good."

"I said peel off them duds," Mad Dog Barton repeated. "If that don't suit your fancy, *I'll* rip them motherlovin' clothes right off you."

Both men sat at the trestle table, watching Rena with the completely focused attention that only naked women and rampaging grizzlies can inspire in men. When Rena still refused to start undressing, Taffy Thomas drew one of his .36 Navy revolvers with tacks all over the hand grips. Her face drained of blood when she realized each tack symbolized a kill.

He tickled his trigger in warning. "Hell, I ain't one to buck the law," he said in a sarcastic tone. "But you're a sporting gal, ain'tcha?"

"No, I am *not*," she retorted hotly.

Mad Dog roared with laughter. "In that case I guess we best tone up our manners, Taffy. This here's a by-god *lady*."

"In a pig's ass. If she acts like a whore, she gets treated like a whore. I s'pose you wasn't doin' the doggy dance with George Winslowe back in Boston, huh? It was writ up in the papers."

"And him a married man," Mad Dog chimed in. "That's a prison crime, so don't try the society-lady skit with us. Peel 'em down so's we can see your tits and your bush."

At the reference to the newspaper story, Rena flushed to the very roots of her hair. Her tormentors laughed and passed the liquor back and forth.

"Black your boots, we're goin' sparkin'!" Taffy exclaimed. "She *is* a whore."

"Sure as shit," Mad Dog said. "Hell, she ain't out here to find no jewels—she's plyin' the carnal trade. You know—workin' her way west."

At this reminder of the jewels, Barton suddenly swung his scattergun up. "This little honey will cut you to wolf bait, trollop. But then, seein's how you was hid in the cabin when I butchered out the Conways, I reckon you know that."

He rose from his seat at the table and stood hip-cocked before her. "The papers are makin' a heap of doin's over them sparklers. Now you tell us where they are."

Rena's mouth was so dry with fear that she had to pry her tongue from the roof of her mouth. "They're hidden right across from Dante's View in a cavern."

Mad Dog's eyes puckered with satisfaction. "That's a good start. Can you take us to 'em?"

"I . . . I can take you to the cavern. I don't know exactly where the jewels are, though."

Both men exchanged a long glance.

"Does your boyfriend know where they are?" Taffy demanded.

"If you mean Skye Fargo . . . he doesn't know and couldn't care less."

"Like hell!" Mad Dog shouted, wagging the barrels of his scattergun for emphasis. "Ain't no man turns his back on easy money like that. Now you tell me the truth or I'll blow you to mattress stuffings. Does that bastard already have those jewels?"

Rena was scared out of her wits, but she also realized the hell that lay in store for her. Anger rose like a tight bubble inside her. The words spurted out before she could stop them.

"Go to hell! I'm done cooperating with you. You're going to murder me anyway, just like you did the Conways. So just go ahead and rape me, then kill me."

"Oh, you'll cooperate," Mad Dog assured her. "A little knifework will see to that. As for the rape part . . ."

He moved in closer, his canine fangs bared. His breathing had grown ragged and loud. "I'll take first whack, Taffy. You step outside and watch for Fargo."

Fargo and Scotty left their mounts hidden behind a pile of scree about a quarter mile north of the shack. Then they clambered over boulders until the shack was visible below them.

"All right," Fargo said, "you stay right on top this boulder. But *stay down*. I'll climb over to the other side and see if I can spot Rena. If I do, I'll point out which end of the shack she's in. When you see me wave my hat, let fly with that smoke pole. Aim for the door if you can."

Fargo laid his Henry atop the boulder. "Remember, as soon as you fire the Big Fifty, ground it and pick up my rifle. Pepper that shack, but avoid the part Rena's in."

Scotty nodded. "I get the easy part. Good luck fishin' her out."

It would indeed be a lot like fishing, Fargo realized as he leaped from boulder to boulder, a coiled lariat in one hand. Rena, too, would be shocked sick and silly when the

Big Fifty opened up. He had to get the rope to her and hope she had enough sense to drop the loop over herself in time for Fargo to haul her up onto the boulders.

He heard voices, mostly masculine and angry, as he sneaked onto a tall, flat-topped boulder at the southwest corner of the shack.

"Like hell!" he heard Mad Dog shout. "Ain't no man turns his back on easy money like that!"

Fargo took a chance and rose to see below into the shack's biggest window. He spotted bright red and his heart surged—the dyed ostrich feather on Rena's straw hat. He caught Scotty's eye and pointed to the side of the shack nearest the valley.

Fargo quickly unlooped a length of the rope. By now Mad Dog's voice was unmistakable: "Oh, you'll cooperate. A little knifework will see to that. . . ."

Fargo waited to hear no more. He waved his hat, and the next second the roar of the Big Fifty echoed down the valley like powerful thunder. Fargo twirled the rope and aimed it right inside the window, the weight of the rope tearing out the remnants of the oiled-paper frame.

Scotty had followed up with the Henry. Fargo, pulse exploding in his ears, watched his rope strike Rena in the back. At first, frozen in fear by the bullets now penetrating the shack, she didn't notice the rope. Anticipating this, Fargo had grabbed a few small stones. He chucked one in, striking her on the shoulder, and finally she glanced outside, then up, and spotted Fargo.

"Grab the rope!" he instructed, mouthing the words and using signals so the owlhoots didn't hear him.

Rena went into action immediately while her captors were busy evading bullets. The moment the loop was set under her arms Fargo began pulling hand over hand. Rena emerged from the window, her face white as new linen.

"Hey! Hey, you bitch, no you don't!"

A brawny arm flew out, reaching for her calico skirt, and Fargo was forced to interrupt his labor long enough to jerk back his Colt and fire. The arm flew inside and, muscles straining like steel cables, Fargo finished pulling Rena up.

"Down!" he shouted, watching a scattergun poke out the window.

Both barrels roared and buckshot caromed off the boulder. Fargo drew his six-gun again and sent several shots through the window.

"C'mon!" he told Rena, leaping to his feet. "We're going up the slope to start a slide, see if we can't bury those two for good."

"Oh, Skye, I never thought you could save me in time!"

"Don't spend it till it's yours, pretty lady," he cautioned as they forged up the slope. "You haven't been rescued yet."

He waved Scotty back, the signal to get clear of the slide area. Fargo knew he had to work fast before Mad Dog and Taffy found their courage and ventured outside. His six-gun would made a poor showing against all their artillery.

"What are you looking for?" Rena asked, watching Fargo cast his eye desperately around them.

"A linchpin. A boulder located just right on the slope to bring plenty more with it."

Fargo made his selection and put his back behind it, straining mightily. The pick was good—almost instantly a huge part of the rocky slope was in motion toward the shack. Unfortunately, Fargo realized too late, the more massive slide caused earlier by Rena had left strategic walls of protection around the shack. Again and again a hurtling boulder that might have smashed the shack to splinters was deflected. When the rumbling slide ended, the shack was undamaged though even more tightly blocked in.

"Well, it was only a plan," Fargo remarked philosophically. "Let's get back to the horses."

As always, he paused long enough to thumb reloads into his Colt.

"This rescue just now," Rena said. "It was magnificent. But it was also just to salve your conscience, right, for letting them get me?"

Fargo laughed, shaking his head in amazement. He could find no sign on the breast of a woman.

"No," he assured her, "it was to save your butt. You want to go back down to the shack?"

"*God* no. You got me out in the nick of time."

Just then a rifle opened up below, and a bullet skipped off a boulder at their feet. Fargo fired on the shack.

"C'mon," he said, taking her hand. "This is no time to recite our coups. We didn't manage to crush those two, and I'm mighty damn sick of 'em. But the worm *will* turn."

"Girl," Scotty told Rena during the ride back to the Conway cabin, "if you looked any lower you'd be walkin' on your lip. You was just rescued, not sentenced to death."

She rode behind Fargo for the short trip and did indeed look despondent. "Oh, don't think I'm ungrateful, Scotty. Both of you were inspiring. It's just—"

She broke off, bitterly disappointed at herself.

"Spit it out," the prospector told her. "You're among friends now."

Rena sighed. "Back at the shack—Mad Dog was about to . . . outrage me. I was desperate to get his mind on something else. So when he brought up the jewels, I more or less told him where they are. But I didn't mention the bottleneck formation."

"How could you tell him where they are?" Fargo put in. "You were unable to find them."

"I told him enough to get them up to the cavern with all those side chambers. They'll be smart enough to look in the right place eventually."

"The hell's all that got to do with the price of tea in China?" Fargo asked.

"I know, I know . . . you said we aren't looking for the jewels anyway. But, Skye, they were the whole point of my trip out here. It's just awful to think about two filthy monsters getting hold of them."

Scotty shook his head. "You're a mighty silly woman, Rena, if you don't think a man like Skye Fargo keeps his word. He already said he'd kill every member of the Barton gang. Three of 'em are already worm castles, and Mad Dog and the redhead will soon be joinin' 'em."

"The way you say," Fargo affirmed. "Whether or not they find those jewels, they'll never get anywhere to sell them. If they end up in our hands, Rena, they'll be sent back special express to the Winslowe family."

"Some consolation," she pouted. "*I've* suffered for them."

Just then, however, Rena lost her pout and smacked a palm against her forehead. "My lands, am I a dunce! I forgot to tell you fellows about the dynamite."

Fargo slewed around in the saddle to look at her. "What dynamite?"

"Three years ago or so they broke into the Grubstake Mine—I forget where it is."

"Was." Scotty corrected her. "It was a deep-rock mine down near the Last Chance Valley south of here."

"Yes, and they broke into the powder magazine and stole some dynamite. They talked about whether it would still be good after being buried here in Death Valley for all that time. Mad Dog thinks it might be good because he wrapped it in wagon canvas."

Fargo looked worried. "Good chance it will still be potent in air this dry. They say when they were going after it?"

"Right away. And Mad Dog mentioned it's a three-hour ride—one way, I think."

"They could have it back here in about six hours." Fargo said, not liking the turn this trail was taking.

"Wouldn't be so bad," Scotty pointed out, "if we was out on the open floor of the valley. But the Conway cabin—hell, after dark one of 'em could flip a stick into the cabin from behind a boulder. Flip a bunch."

Fargo nodded. "Hate to say it, but we best move again."

"Out into the open valley?" Rena asked. "Our very first camp fills the bill."

"It does," Fargo agreed. "But then we're right back to the cat-and-mouse game, and who knows when they'll even find us? I prefer bringing all this to a head, the sooner the better. That means going someplace where we know they'll be coming."

Rena looked stunned. "You don't mean . . . ?"

"Sure. The cavern up in the mountains near Dante's View. It's not open and flat, but it's high ground with only one trail in. I say we head up there and let our greedy enemies come to us."

"Skye, you can't see Rena grinnin' behind you," Scotty complained. "But she's already got them jewels in her mind."

"That point's already been settled," Fargo said amiably. "It's dynamite and killers we'd best be watching for, not flubdubs in a box."

18

"The thing is," Scotty gleefully reminded Rena, "thanks to that newspaper, the whole damn country knows you're out here to lay hands on them jewels. You don't dare take 'em now."

"I do if I'm not afraid to disappear," she retorted, unable to see Scotty behind her on the steep trail. "There's still places the law can't find."

"The woman has lost her buttons," Scotty announced to the sterile, waterless mountain. "She'll soon run her own road gang."

They were only fairly started before Scotty, who hated forced sobriety, had begun to harass Rena. Fargo shifted his shell belt so he could slew around in the saddle and study the lifeless floor of Death Valley, about four-thousand feet below them. A long look through his field glasses showed no one in the afternoon glare.

"All clear?" Rena asked.

"Looks that way. Good bet Mad Dog and the redhead are still digging up their dynamite. We might get up there unseen."

Rena said, "Skye, you've dealt with plenty of criminals. What makes men like Mad Dog Barton the way they are?"

Fargo shook his head. "Ask somebody who reads skull bumps. Me, I figure there's just a hole in them somewheres."

"They're a fox-eared tribe," Scotty put in. "No mis-doubting that."

Fargo did know one thing—the images of the slaughtered and desecrated Conway family would cling in his memory like a burr to wool.

"Speakin' of somethin' missing," Scotty interjected, "what about water up topside, Skye? The canteens and gutbag are all full, but two horses and a mule will need plenty."

"My last trip, I noticed seepage in the cave," Fargo replied. "Might be water inside the place." Luckily his Ovaro had been fed up on oats and corn before Fargo headed north, anticipating poor fodder.

"No tellin' what we might find up there," Scotty complained, "now that the story about the jewels has been noised about."

Rena tugged the Smith and Wesson from her pannier—since Skye had given it to her it never left her reach.

"There's no clue in that newspaper story," Fargo reminded them, "that tells anybody where to start looking. Now both of you cinch up your lips—we're cutting across the saddle that leads to the cavern. The last stretch of trail is narrow and steep. Be ready for anything."

Fargo knew that, at his angle, bucking, jackknifing, and crow-hopping could be lethal on this narrow trail. But he trusted his stallion, loosening the reins and giving the Ovaro his head. At the final approach Fargo drew his Colt, but the area around the bottleneck formation appeared deserted.

The view below was not as spectacular as from nearby Dante's View, but Fargo was impressed—it was so open to the east that a man could almost see tomorrow.

"Never thought I'd say it," Fargo admitted as he tossed the reins forward and swung down, "but I'd welcome the sight of a plank walk and even a few city whippersnappers."

Despite knowing the two outlaws couldn't be up here yet, Fargo stepped carefully into the first cavern and looked around. Well lighted near the entrance, it grew rapidly darker a few yards within.

"Be darker than the inside of a boot after sundown," Scotty complained.

"I've got stubs of candle in my saddle, old roadster," Fargo said. "But we *will* miss those cornhusk mattresses at the cabin."

"It's amazing," Rena said, "but counting our first night's camp in Death Valley, this is the fourth hideout we've used since Mad Dog Barton first clashed with us."

"Humph," Scotty grunted. "We're all still alive, ain't we?

And Skye has trimmed their numbers considerable. Not a one of them has escaped bein' shot or killed."

"Yeah, but his new threat is dynamite," Fargo cautioned. "We best hark to the signs, all of us. When you're on guard, say little and miss nothing. They'll figure out quick where we are, and though that trail's narrow, once they get up here there's places to spread out and hide."

Despite the more desperate terrain of this prolonged encounter, it struck Fargo as a typical frontier battle: no laurels to be won, just a hard, bloody contest for survival.

Rena had drifted away, and Fargo knew she was searching for the now famous cherrywood box. She returned, however, with an armload of dead firewood.

"One of the chambers is filled with this," she marveled. "Who could have brought it up here, and from where?"

"It's most likely from the east slope of the Sierras," Fargo said. "Whoever did it knows deadwood doesn't smoke. Could've been Mohaves, maybe, and there's Paiutes close by."

"It's cooler up here than down below," Rena said, "but could they possibly have needed heat?"

"Cooking and light," Fargo guessed. "Feel all the breezes in here? This place has natural vents. We can keep a fire going nights, well away from the entrance."

Two hours later the sun didn't set—it just suddenly seemed to collapse and it was night. The thick rock, and mile-high altitude, did turn the air much cooler. Soon the cave was sweet with the smell of burning wood.

With Scotty on guard outside the cave and Fargo busy cleaning weapons, Rena again struck out to look for the box of jewelry. The large fire they'd built sent illumination into many of the chambers, large and small, that formed off the main cavern.

Rena's sudden, shrill scream brought both men running, six-guns cocked for action. Fargo found her about thirty yards from the main entrance, almost babbling with hysteria.

"My *God*," she managed, pointing a trembling finger into a small room. *"Look!"*

Scotty made a choking sound and turned away, on the verge of retching. Fargo, however, was riveted by fascination and revulsion.

There was enough firelight to show he was staring into

a scorpion pit, with hundreds of the poisonous creatures writhing all over each other.

"You were lucky," Fargo remarked, glancing down at the floor of the room. Had Rena stepped into the chamber, there was a sudden drop of five feet or so into the writhing black mass.

"But, Skye," she said, horrified. "We have to kill them, or how can we stay here?"

"No need to kill them. Have you seen any of them anyplace but here? They must have water down there or they couldn't reproduce in such numbers."

"The hell they doin' for food?" Scotty asked.

"Take a closer look," Fargo replied. "The healthy ones are eating the sick and old."

Rena made a strange sound and turned quickly away. "My God! One more step, and *I* would have been the meal."

"Yeah," Fargo said thoughtfully, "just step in and fall— a fitting fate for a woman killer."

Scotty grunted. "How would you get Mad Dog to go in here?"

"We'd have to shake the oat bag a little, but he could be lured," Fargo replied, slanting a glance toward Rena.

"Rena," Scotty said in a teasing tone as the three moved back out to the main chamber, "what if them jewels're hidden in this room? Scorpions might not've been here when they was hid."

"Oh, shut up," she snapped.

"Never mind the scorpions," Fargo told Scotty. "Mad Dog and Taffy could be on their way up here. Instead of running your mouth at a 2:40 clip, get back out front and watch that trail up."

All the way back from Last Chance Canyon, spurs with four-inch rowels kept Mad Dog and Taffy's horses running hard. Both mounts were lathered and blowing hard by the time they reached the mouth of Grapevine Canyon.

It was dark, but a bright white full moon and thousands of stars scattered broadcast showed the luminous outline of the Conway cabin.

"Might be asleep by now," Taffy suggested. "Place is dark."

"Even so, Fargo or the old prospector will be on guard," Mad Dog said. "We'll hobble the horses here and sneak up on foot. Each of us will flip two sticks at the cabin. That should blow it to smithereens."

"What if we kill the sketchin' bitch?" Taffy asked. "She owes us a poke, and besides, she's our ticket to the sparklers."

"Yeah, but it's more important for us to avoid hangin' than it is to get rich. Besides, I been thinkin' on it—seems to me they might already have them jewels with 'em. If so, they'll likely survive the explosion."

"But, Mad Dog, if they got the sparklers, why would they hang around here?"

Barton shook his head. "Fargo's a crusader, and there's no law out here in Death Valley. I think he means to put the quietus on us for killin' the Conways. But to hell with all that. Let's just kill all three of them."

He reached into a saddlebag and removed four sticks of dynamite. They had already crimped blasting caps and short fuses to each stick of stabilized nitro. Mad Dog handed two sticks to Taffy.

"You hook around to the west end of the cabin. I'll take the east," he said. "Fargo is sharp, so move in slow and stay among the boulders. Got lucifers?"

"Yeah. Let's get it done. I'm sick of this mother-ruttin' valley."

Mad Dog nodded. "All right, wait for my first toss, then throw yours. If Fargo is outside and wants to chuck lead, we'll both unlimber on him."

For the next half hour or so Mad Dog carefully leap-frogged himself into a good spot in boulders near the cabin. He had not spotted a sentry once, which made him nervous. It was nothing so easy to lay the tongue to, but he sensed they were being snookered by Fargo yet again.

He scratched a match to life on a boulder, lit the fuse of his first stick, and hurled it up against the foundation of the cabin. The blast lit up the night and sent sand and debris slapping against his protective boulder. Three more flashes followed, in quick succession, as he and Taffy hurled the rest of their dynamite.

The cabin lay in complete ruins, shattered logs burning.

Carrying one of his scatterguns, Mad Dog crept forward. "Taffy?"

"Yo?"

"Spot any sentry?"

"No, and that don't make sense."

Yeah it does, Mad Dog fretted, *if they left the cabin.*

With three people, two horses, and a mule supposed to be inside the cabin, it should have been easy to spot a corpse or part of one. But a frenzied search of the rubble failed to turn up a trace of them.

"God*damn*it," Mad Dog shouted, adding a choice string of curses. "Fargo flimflammed us again."

"Mad Dog!" Taffy exclaimed, his voice close to panic. "You don't think Fargo and them left Death Valley while we was diggin' up the dynamite? They'll go right to law if they did."

Mad Dog mulled it. "Nah. If Fargo stuck it out this long, he's still around."

"But where?"

Mad Dog stared east toward the dark mass of the Black Mountains, his face closed and bitter. "There's no good places left down here on the bed. But if you wanted high ground—*and*, just maybe, a fortune in jewels—where would you head?"

"Maybe that cavern the bitch mentioned, the one just to the right of Dante's View," Taffy replied.

"Let's water the horses and head up there."

Both men trotted back to their mounts and removed the hobbles. Mad Dog stepped up into leather and yanked his sorrel around toward Furnace Creek.

"Fargo's probably laughing up his sleeve over those explosions," he said just before he sank steel into his mount. "But you mark my words, Taffy—we *will* dance on his bones!"

147

19

It was nearing eleven p.m. by Scotty's vest-pocket watch, and Fargo had just started his first stint of guard duty in front of the cavern. He had a good view of the solitary, narrow trail leading over to the bottleneck-shaped sandstone formation.

He had selected a bench rock about twenty feet outside the cavern entrance. Enough firelight leaked outside the cavern to mark it, and Fargo insisted on that—light usually favored the attacked, not the attackers.

His Henry lay across his thighs, and he had spent much of his time sharpening his Arkansas toothpick. He expected Mad Dog and Taffy to pay a visit to the Conway cabin tonight, and sure enough, shortly after Fargo relieved Scotty, four closely spaced explosions rose up from Grapevine Canyon.

Rena, stripped down to her thin chemise at Fargo's request, came running outside. Scotty was still dressed from guard duty, and he ambled out behind her.

"Well, Skye," Scotty said after taking a long size-up of Rena's near-naked body, "that answers you the question 'bout their dynamite still bein' good."

"So that's what it was?" Rena asked.

Fargo grinned at the scantily clad woman. She was clutching her elbows in nervousness. "You're the one who warned us about the dynamite, Boston belle."

"I know, but it did give my heart a jupe to hear it. The cabin, you think?"

"Where else?" Fargo asked.

"Mebbe we'll get lucky," Scotty suggested. "They might think they killed us."

148

"Not likely," Fargo gainsaid. "Dynamite wouldn't pulverize a corpse, and they won't even find one of us."

Rena said, "Well, anyway, I bet they have more."

Fargo remained calmly seated. "Sure they do."

Rena watched the trail and the inky fathoms of darkness. "Think we're next?"

"We'd be fools to think otherwise. They saw us come up this way before today, and besides, they know the jewels are up here somewhere."

"Can we beat two men—*clever* men," Rena emphasized, "who are armed with dynamite?"

"If they're so damned clever," Fargo teased her, "why did they just waste four sticks of explosives on an empty cabin?"

"She's just buryin' us again," Scotty barbed. "That's her favorite pastime."

"Why don't both of you turn in?" Fargo suggested. "I'm s'posed to be on guard duty here, not jawboning all holler under the stars."

They took his advice, and Fargo spent the next two hours mostly patrolling down the trail, occasionally sitting in front of the cavern to rest. When he heard the Ovaro whinny, he stepped into complete shadows.

He knew something was coming, but nonetheless, he flinched violently when Mad Dog's voice suddenly split the still darkness, seeming like a disembodied voice on the mountain.

"Fargo! Prepare yourself to die, boy!"

Fargo heard whispering footsteps from the cavern behind him.

"Stay there!" he called in a harsh whisper. "You're safer."

"Hear me, Trailsman?" Mad Dog's voice growled. "You're going to die tonight!"

"You got it hindside foremost," Fargo corrected him. "*You're* going to die—like a dog. A mad dog."

During all this Fargo tried to get an ear location on the speaker as well as some location on the redhead. The voice did not come from the trail, but from the jumble of cover to the left of it. The terrain up here was difficult to move around in, but provided plenty of hiding places for men and horses.

"Fargo!" Mad Dog's voice roared out again—he had shifted to a new location. "We got a stick with your name on it. It's gonna blow you to trap bait. But we ain't gonna waste your little honey who wallows with married men. We're gonna make her see God before we kill her."

"You know, Mad Dog," Fargo said calmly, "I never met a coward yet who didn't use words and threats to stand in for his manhood. If you're in fighting fettle, then come out of hiding like a man and let's get thrashing. Short guns, fists, knives, you call it."

Fargo heard a muffled curse. Moments later, a stick of dynamite spitting sparks came arcing over the boulders and landed in the clearing. Fargo ducked behind his boulder as an ear-numbing explosion threw debris everywhere.

"Chew on that, Fargo!" Barton taunted.

"Just a lot of harmless noise, Mad Dog, like you."

Another stick came twirling in, but this time Fargo was ready to gamble. He leaped forward, grabbed it off the ground on the run, and flipped it underhanded in the same direction from which it had come. The explosion was muffled by all the boulders it landed among.

"Chew on that," Fargo taunted.

Just then, however, he found out where Taffy was as a rifle opened up, slugs swarming around Fargo. Spotting streaks of muzzle flash, he dropped to one knee and rained fury with the Henry. Fargo's bullets whanged from rock to rock, silencing the shooter.

"Think you got 'em, Skye?" Scotty called from the cavern.

"Nah, neither one unless I was awful lucky. But I hear 'em both retreating."

The rest of Fargo's stint was uneventful. Scotty took over for the final stretch until sunrise.

"Don't wander too far from the cave," Fargo advised. "That dynamite's too easy to flip inside. So keep your six-gun to hand. If you see or hear anything, fire your short gun to warn me."

Scotty sat just outside the entrance to see better, his ears and eyes vigilant. The moon deepened from ivory to butter yellow as the night advanced to the last hours before dawn—which sailors called the dog watch and Scotty renamed the Mad Dog watch.

The silence—no insect hum even—was eerie. Scotty removed a plug of eating tobacco from his trousers and carved off a chaw. When he had the "suption" just right, he cheeked his cud.

Scotty thought he heard the scrape of boot leather and stared out into the surrounding darkness. A heartbeat later a rock bounced off his forehead, and Scotty grunted, consciousness rapidly ebbing. With the last of his awareness he heard a sinister, familiar sound like a fuse catching fire.

Even as blackness overwhelmed him, Scotty recalled Fargo's order: *If you see or hear anything, fire your short gun to warn me.*

Something spitting orange sparks rocketed toward the cave. Scotty curled his index finger around the trigger, and the same moment he pulled it he slumped to the ground, dead to the world.

After years spent on dangerous trails, Fargo always woke instantly, ready for action. At the sudden crack of Scotty's Remington, he sat up, drawing his Colt. Before he even had time to grasp the situation, a stick of burning dynamite hurtled through the entrance.

By reflex, not thought, he dropped his Colt and, willing himself steady, sprang up to catch the dynamite in midair. Knowing Scotty was out there somewhere, he heaved it hard, and the resulting explosion rocked the ground and rained debris everywhere.

He and Rena charged out of the cave, six-guns blazing. Fargo heard cursing followed by the sounds of a clumsy, hasty retreat.

"Scotty!" Rena exclaimed, spotting his slumped form. "Is he . . . ?"

"He just took a nasty conk on the noggin," Fargo told her, retrieving his canteen and splashing water on the prospector. "Long way from his heart. But the tough old stallion got a warning shot off before he blacked out. He saved both of us, Rena—that dynamite would've painted the walls with us."

Scotty's eyes fluttered open. "Christ, Skye, hurts somethin' fierce. I never once seen 'em," he apologized.

"You're a credit to your dam, old-timer," Fargo said in praise. "Soon as you can, go back inside and get some sleep. I'll take over for the rest of the night."

Fargo suspected that two failed attempts in one night would be enough to dampen the enemy's kill fever for now, and he was right—dawn broke over the east California desert with no further attacks.

Scotty woke up with a pounding headache and a lump the size of an egg on his forehead. They had coffee again now, thanks to the Conway larder, and the cavern was aromatic with its smell.

"Found this last night," Scotty said, showing Fargo an arrowhead of flaked flint. "Mohave?"

Fargo shrugged. He sat near the entrance so he could watch things outside. "At one time the California tribes numbered in the thousands. The gold rush destroyed a lot of them."

Scotty shook his head. "I don't know about Injins. I knew a Modoc that had him a flintlock. Thought he could save powder, so he charged the piece light. When the bullets dropped short or bounced off the game, he threw the damn gun away."

"Or they overload the gun," Fargo said, "and blow their faces off."

Rena rose to her feet. "This is all very stimulating, but I think I'll explore the chambers a bit more while the sunlight is coming straight in."

"Why bother?" Scotty roweled her, giving her a mulish expression. "Skye's already told you you're not stealing the jewels."

"I want to see them," Rena shot back. "And perhaps the Winslowes will offer a reward for their return."

"Bull," Scotty told Fargo after she left. "She means to leave the box behind and stuff the play-pretties into her, ahh, secret places."

Fargo waved off the topic. "I'm more worried about the horses and General Washington. They need stalls and clean straw if they're going to be kept inside, and we're low on oats. Like I've said all along: We need to push this fight to a showdown."

"That shines, but how? Christ, they got dynamite now."

Fargo nodded. "And it looks like they've given up on the jewels or else they'd try to spare Rena. They just want us dead before we report the Conway murders. Still . . . might be a way to end this thing."

Scotty perked up. "You got a plan?"

"Nothing too fancy. But usually simple is best."

"Fargo!" Mad Dog's hidden voice abruptly shouted from somewhere outside. "Sleep a little rough last night?"

"Got more sleep than you did," Fargo assured him. "You're the one staying in constant motion and using dynamite instead of guns. Where's it got you?"

"You're challenging *me* with guns, you lanky son of a bitch? You must be the joker in this deck. Let's square off for a draw-shoot and see what a big man you are."

"Suits me right down to the ground," Fargo said calmly. "I'm ready now."

Clearly Mad Dog had carried his bluff too far, expecting Fargo to be dead set against a walk-and-draw, nor was he even confident that he could beat Fargo. There was a long pause, then:

"Ahh, I twig your game, Trailsman. You *say* it'll be a draw-shoot, but you'll try a fox play. You're not a gunfighter."

"The words mean nothing. If it pounds nails it's a hammer. And so far I've hammered three members of your gang. Won't be long, I'll hammer the other two."

"Save your brags for somebody who gives a shit. Fargo, either you bend with the breeze or you break. Me 'n' Taffy are gettin' bored, and we got an offer: Give us the woman and the old man and we'll let you go."

Fargo saw their reasoning immediately. Rena and Scotty were eyewitnesses to the Conway killings, whereas Fargo only knew about the crime from hearsay.

"You'll let me go?" Fargo repeated. "Mad Dog, case you haven't noticed, nobody's got me. I'm a free-range maverick. I'm here by my own choice, and after I kill the two of you I'll ride on."

"Don't blow smoke up my ass, mouthpiece! You had your chance! Now you're gonna buy the farm, bull and all!"

20

"I think you ruffled the man's feathers, Skye," Scotty opined.

Fargo resumed his careful watch. "He's a lot of swamp gas, but I hear they're both dead shots with a six-gun."

"Used to was, you never heard about 'gunmen,' jaspers who practice killin' themselves in mirrors. These two don't seem too eager to brace you, Skye."

"Fine by me—Mad Dog, especially, doesn't deserve that quick a death. He deserves the *paso de la muerte*."

"I only speak two languages," Scotty told him. "American and cussin'. The hell'd you just say?"

"It means something like 'the stunt of death,' " Fargo explained. "Mad Dog pulled the triggers in the Conway cabin, so he deserves an especially horrifying death."

"Hell, that's jim-dandy just so it's ended."

"They'll come a cropper," Fargo predicted. "And soon."

"Dang well better. And before too many more sticks of dynamite are tossed at us."

After careful study of the surroundings, Fargo slowly ventured out of the cave. He still had not discovered a water source despite obvious damp spots within the cavern and its related chambers.

"Stay inside," he told Scotty, studying the ground intently.

"The hell you lookin' for?"

"Water. I can usually find some in rock hollows, but it's yet to rain this year. I've seen the occasional seep holding water in the desert, but I've never found groundwater in dead mountains like these. Has to be some here, though."

"I found it," Rena's voice announced as she joined

154

Scotty near the cave entrance. "It's in a chamber so far back it's pitch-dark. But I found it—a little stone cistern with flowing water going through it."

Fargo went back with her and tasted the water, finding it clear and fresh. All three mounts were watered in turn, two armed guards at the cave entrance at all times.

"Say, Boston princess," Scotty spoke up when the watering was finished, "found your box of sparklers yet?"

"Is this the face of an ecstatic woman?" she jeered.

Scotty snorted. "I'd look scratchy, too, if my unmentionables was stuffed full of jewels."

"The unmitigated gall! Who do you—"

"Turn off the tap," Fargo snapped. "You two better cooperate. I'm riding out for a little while, and with two hidebound killers out there, we can't fight amongst ourselves."

"Riding where?" Rena demanded. "And why?"

"I need to take a good squint around," Fargo replied. "Even when it's risky I like to scout. Besides, these killers only get braver if we hide from 'em. Best to let 'em know who rules the roost."

Fargo rigged his stallion and rode out, left arm holding the brass-framed Henry. He skipped the trail and rode behind the bottleneck formation, where the actual top of the mountain reached its full height.

Fargo usually climbed a tree when he wanted to see the bigger picture; on a mountain devoid of growth, however, a tumble of boulders was the best option. He worked his way slowly upward until he'd cleared the obstructing heaps of scree and moraine for an impressive view. Death Valley lay bone white and empty just below him, but Fargo spotted greasewood cactus in the desert surrounding the valley.

A rifle shot cracked into the stillness, and rock dust puffed up less than a foot from his right hand. Follow-on shots—all from high-powered rifles—made Fargo scramble down in leaps, showing impressive athleticism. Not, however, before glimpsing a reddish-gold horse hidden east of him.

"Let's get out of the weather, boy," he urged his stallion.

Fargo swung aboard just as a new flurry of shots opened up. The Ovaro hunkered on his hocks, lowering Fargo's profile. When the volley trailed off, the pinto sprang forward while Fargo tossed lead in the direction of the hidden

155

horse. It must have surprised Mad Dog and Taffy, because their rifles fell silent.

Either they were out of dynamite or Fargo was past their range. But as he rounded the mountain peak he reminded himself it was time to step on two roaches once and for all.

Until well past midnight Mad Dog and Taffy watched the cavern entrance with its ruby red sheen from a fire within.

"They're not even posting a sentry," Mad Dog whispered. "Think they scared us last night. Hell, I can make out three bedrolls even, a sleeper in every one."

"I don't trust Fargo any farther than I can throw him," Taffy insisted. "It's a trick."

"We'll pitch this in first," Mad Dog assured him, wagging a stick of dynamite.

"Toss it past the horses near the entrance," Taffy said. "That pinto of Fargo's is worth a small fortune."

Sticking to the shadows, both men crept closer, the sounds of advance covered by the howling of constant wind. Mad Dog gave the high sign. While Taffy held both Navy Colts cocked and ready, Mad Dog fired the fuse, held the dynamite a few seconds, and lobbed it into the middle of the bedrolls.

Both men leaped aside just before a roaring belch of fire and a wall of blast debris shot from the cavern. Taffy rushed into the smoking inferno first, ready to kill anything that moved. He advanced perhaps four steps before the oak warclub bristling with spikes killed him in one lethal blow that punctured his brain.

Fargo had hidden in a niche just inside the entrance, safe from the blast. The warclub had been used to avoid alerting Mad Dog. Quickly Fargo dragged the body aside, feet still twitching, just before Barton followed his partner in.

"Get ready, hon," Fargo whispered to Rena.

The fire had not been destroyed in the blast, and Mad Dog Barton spotted Rena, who was still pulling on her chemise, disappearing in a rear passage. A quick glimpse of her ivory derriere seemed to mesmerize him.

Fargo had guessed these woman-starved men wouldn't kill Rena unless they had to, and Barton never fired a shot at her.

"Taffy!" he shouted. "Taffy! You all right?"

"Yeah!" replied a voice, muffled by so much rock. "Fargo's dead, and I'm lookin' for the old fart!"

Fargo heard Mad Dog chuckle. "Dead, huh? The big crusader. All right, sketchin' bitch, spread them legs for your new man."

Fargo followed, Colt in his right fist, as Mad Dog slipped from chamber to chamber, the light dimming as he moved farther back. Fargo watched him practically leap into a room, and then a surprised grunt was followed by a solid impact as he landed.

"What the—? Jesus! What . . . oh, God Almighty!"

At first Mad Dog bawled like a bay steer. By the time Fargo, Scotty, and Rena reached the dimly lighted scorpion pit, however, his screams of fear, pain, and revulsion were ear-piercing. One sting, Fargo knew, would only make an adult male feel miserable for a few hours. Three or four stings were fatal, and by now scores of scorpions had injected their tail stingers into Mad Dog.

Fargo watched him writhe and scream in terrified agony, feeling no pity for this flint-hearted butcher of women.

Scotty watched Mad Dog disappear under a living black blanket of smothering death. It was the prospector's voice that had lured Barton back here with the report that Fargo was dead.

"Won't need to worry about Barton's body," he remarked. "But the redhead is layin' out there bold as a big man's ass, his brains in his hair. Should we bury him?"

"I bury no man who tries to kill me," Fargo replied. "That's a rule with me."

Scotty grinned. "I got a rule, too. Never get caught on the blister end of a shovel. We'll toss his blanket over him—we won't be here long anyhow."

"Your *paso de la muerte* worked to perfection," Rena told Fargo. "But I wasted my time with this entire trip. Those jewels are nowhere inside these caves. Somebody found them."

Fargo nodded. "Just as well. Tomorrow we leave Death Valley and head east through the Tehachapi Pass to the San Fernando Valley. Then you can head home."

"Maybe," Rena speculated, "the jewels are still—"

"I wouldn't put one red penny on it," Fargo interrupted her. "You just be ready to leave in the morning."

*   *   *

Several days of easy, uneventful riding brought them into the fertile, blessedly cool San Fernando Valley. Grass grew up to the stirrups in places, and they were surrounded by mountain slopes bristling with conifers. It bothered Fargo, however, to spot several surveyors with their theodolites. Behind their lines of survey stakes would come graders, track-bed crews, and track layers.

"Now *that's* a proper way station," Rena remarked, pointing ahead to a building with a wide verandah. It was made of adobe plastered white with a red tile roof. A livery barn of new slab lumber sat behind it.

"Let's rein in," Fargo suggested. "Food might be good, and our mounts need a good feed."

The place did indeed seem opulent after a stint in rustic Death Valley. There was a starling in a wooden cage. Rena stroked the oilcloth on their table as if it were fine French muslin, and all three fell raptly silent when a female customer played "My Old Kentucky Home" on a small upright piano.

While they tied into delicious steaks, Fargo said to Rena, "I know why you never found those jewels."

She set down her fork. "Do tell?"

Fargo nodded. "I found them first. So I tossed them off the face of the mountain. We didn't need the trouble."

Rena sent Fargo a look that knifed him. Even Scotty nearly choked on his food.

"A lot of money down a rat hole," Rena said in a wooden voice. "*That's* what you tossed away."

"Yep," Fargo admitted cheerfully. "Right down a rat hole."

Rena stared, unable to give voice to her conflicting emotions. Then, suddenly, she shocked Fargo and Scotty by bursting into unrestrained laughter. She couldn't stop herself, which made Scotty and Fargo catch the belly-laughers, too. Before long, every patron in the place was teary-eyed from the infectious mirth.

"Skye," she said when she finally had herself under control, "if it hadn't been for you saving my life so many times, I'd've been killed before I ever found the jewels. They were lost to me anyway. The coals of that dream have turned to ash. I'm just happy to be alive."

"That's all I need to hear," Fargo told her.

His saddlebags were draped in a pile beside his chair. Fargo untied one and pulled a small cherrywood box out, setting it in front of Rena. Her eyes went huge and white, and she seemed afraid to touch it. The tip of her tongue eased out to lick her dry lips.

"Skye, do you mean—is this *it*?"

"All I know is, I found this box on the first day we all moved into the cavern. It was hidden behind some rocks in the corner of one of the rooms."

"But you were high-minded and swore you'd never take the Winslowe jewels."

"Both you two put a stopper on your gobs," Scotty cut in, his voice impatient. "Ain't nobody can see us from here, Skye. Open that box. I ain't never seed diamonds and such."

Fargo slid open the clasp and raised the lid. Scotty and Rena stared, so surprised and confused that Fargo had to clear his throat to remind them they had tongues.

Rena recovered first. She couldn't tear her eyes away from the small white rocks filling the box, all beautifully painted in intricate designs.

"Why, they're exquisite," she said. "Some are just like the miniature portraits that were all the rage in Elizabethan England. But these depict Indians."

"Several desert tribes make them," Fargo said. "My guess is that an Indian or Indians found the jewels, realized they were valuable, and took them, leaving the painted stones in trade."

"Say," Scotty said, "I've seen stones like them for sale in San Francisco. They come dear, too."

"Imagine how dear they'd be in Boston," Rena said, her eyes calculating. "But I'd need to hire a dependable man to chaperone me back east—would you take the job, Scotty?"

"*Me?*"

"Of course. Skye thinks highly of you, and so do I."

Scotty hitched his belt up. "I reckon the Front Range can wait a spell. A gentleman should always help a lady. Ain't that right, Skye?"

Fargo grinned through his somewhat neglected beard. His eyes met Rena's. "Right as rain. A gent should always aim to please a lady."

"That's very nice to hear," she replied. "Especially since we have one more night on the trail 'before we reach the mission."

Fargo removed his hat and looked pious. For a man who felt a permanent urge to push on, over the next ridge, girls like Rena were timely met.

"Duty calls," he said, "and the Trailsman must obey."

LOOKING FORWARD!

**The following is the opening
section of the next novel in the exciting
Trailsman series from Signet:**

THE TRAILSMAN #305
WYOMING WIPEOUT

*Fort Laramie, 1858—there's a dangerous gang of
stagecoach robbers on the loose along the mail
route, and only the Trailsman can stop them. If they
don't kill him first.*

Skye Fargo wasn't looking for a job. He'd just gotten into
St. Joseph, and he had a little money to spend. He figured
on staying in town and enjoying himself for a day or so
before looking for some pilgrims to escort along the Oregon Trail, out to Fort Laramie, Fort Bridger, or all the way
to Oregon if that was what they wanted.

So when the little man in dude's clothes showed up at
his elbow, Fargo told him to go away.

"I'm afraid I can't do that," the man said. He might have
been a little fella, but he had a big voice that carried well
in the noisy room. "You *are* Skye Fargo, aren't you? The
one they call the Trailsman?"

Fargo was tempted to lie, but he didn't think it would do any good. He said, "That's me."

"And I am Samuel Dobkins. You are the man I am looking for."

Dobkins had a soft, round face and a thick black mustache. He wore white checked pants and a purple checked frock coat. On his head was a straw topper with a black band. The hat added nearly a foot to his inconsiderable height. He didn't look like anybody who'd be interested in a trip to Oregon.

"I don't know you," Fargo said, hoping Dobkins would go away.

Dobkins didn't leave. He touched the brim of his topper and said, "Mr. Ferriday wants to talk to you."

Fargo was more interested in the glass of whiskey on the table in front of him than in somebody named Mr. Ferriday. He said so.

"Mr. J. M. Ferriday," Dobkins said.

Fargo shook his head. The name was familiar, but he wasn't interested in talking to anyone. "I still don't care."

"That's neither here nor there," the dude said. "The fact remains that you simply must go talk to Mr. Ferriday. At once."

Fargo sighed and looked around the saloon. Men laughed and talked at the tables, and a couple of card games were going on near the wall to one side. The bar was lined with men who had nowhere better to go and nothing better to do. Fargo wished he was one of them instead of one who was sitting there talking to Dobkins.

"Show's starting in a few minutes," Fargo said, gesturing toward the tiny stage at the rear of the big room. "I'm planning to see it."

"You can return this evening," Dobkins told him. "There will be another show."

Fargo took a drink of his whiskey. It was bad whiskey, but it was better than no whiskey at all. He set the glass back on the table and said, "I don't want to come back this evening, and I don't want to talk to Mr. Ferriday. Now light a shuck."

Dobkins straightened his shoulders and tugged at his coat to straighten it. He opened his mouth, but he didn't have a chance to say anything because a large snaggle-toothed man with a mug of beer in each hand walked by and deliberately knocked off his hat with one elbow.

The man laughed loudly and went on his way. Dobkins picked up his hat, dusted it off, and set it firmly on his head.

"Excuse me, Mr. Fargo," he said, turning to follow the man who'd knocked off his hat.

The man was about to sit down at a table with three others when Dobkins caught up with him.

"You did that deliberately," Dobkins said.

Setting the beer mugs on the table, Snaggle-tooth turned to face him. "Yeah? And so what if I did?"

He was a good foot taller than Dobkins, even counting the topper. Dobkins looked at him for a second and then kicked him in the knee. The man wasn't bothered any more than if a mosquito had bitten him. He swept Dobkins's hat off with a hand the size of a frying pan. The hat sailed a couple of feet and hit the floor near another table.

Dobkins went over to pick up the hat. When he reached for it, Snaggle-tooth crushed it to the floor with his foot.

Dobkins whirled and slammed a fist into the man's groin. The man buckled, and Dobkins head-butted him, smashing his nose. Blood flew.

The man's three friends jumped up from the table and lunged at Dobkins. All around, people shoved back their chairs and tables and got out of the way, ready to watch Dobkins get dismembered.

Fargo sighed. It wasn't his fight, and it wasn't his fault, but he didn't feel he could sit by and watch Dobkins get beaten. Dobkins had come there looking for him, after all, and the little man had grit.

Fargo hoped Dobkins's attackers would listen to reason, but just in case they wouldn't, he pulled his .45.

"I don't allow any gunplay in here," the bartender said at Fargo's back.

Fargo glanced around. The bartender held a shotgun, and it was pointed at the Trailsman.

"They'll tear the place up," Fargo said.

The bartender shrugged, but the gun remained steady. "If they do, they'll pay for it. Now holster that hogleg."

Fargo did as he was told. By that time Dobkins was at the bottom of a pile of squirming men and flying fists.

"Be all right if I joined in?" Fargo said.

The bartender grinned. "Be my guest."

The snaggle-toothed man who'd started the whole thing was in a dither. He didn't know whether to hold his bleeding nose or his injured gonads. Fargo shoved him to a seat in an empty chair and pulled one man off the pile. The man windmilled his arms in an attempt to hit Fargo, but the Trailsman avoided the futile blows. He took the man by the shirtfront and belt and heaved him over a table. He hit headfirst on the floor, rolled over, and was still.

A second man jumped up and grabbed a chair. He broke it across Fargo's back before the Trailsman could turn around. Fargo stumbled forward and fell into the table that he'd tossed the man over. The table collapsed under his weight. The men sitting there just scooted their chairs back out of the way as the man pounced for Fargo.

The Trailsman flipped over before the man reached him and got his hands up in time to put them around the man's throat. The man's fingers gouged at Fargo's eyes, but Fargo's grip tightened. The man's face reddened and his breath rasped, then whistled, then stopped. His hands fell limp, and Fargo pushed him aside.

When he stood up, he was surprised to see Dobkins standing over the third man. Dobkins held the leg of the chair that had been broken across Fargo's back in both hands like a club, and he must have used it like one. The man's hair hung bloody and matted over his forehead.

As Fargo watched, Dobkins tossed the chair leg on the man's chest and dusted himself off. He straightened his frock coat and looked around for his hat. When he saw it, he bent over and picked it up. He shook it off and punched it out with his fist. It was battered and dirty, but Dobkins put it on.

The snaggle-tooth who'd started it all still sat in the chair where Fargo had pushed him. He held a dirty cloth to his bloody nose and had one hand in his crotch.

Fargo walked back to his table and tossed down the rest of his whiskey. He put down the glass and saw that Dobkins was standing beside him.

"Are you ready to go, Mr. Fargo?" Dobkins said.

"I'm not going."

"After all my trouble? You certainly are."

Fargo started to repeat his previous comment when he felt something jab his side. Glancing down he saw that Dobkins was poking a derringer into his ribs.

"Well?" Dobkins said.

"I guess I might as well go with you," Fargo said.

Dobkins nodded. "I thought you might. After you, Mr. Fargo."

Fargo led the way toward the door. Just before he pushed through the batwings, the bartender called to them.

"Who's paying for the damages?"

Dobkins gestured over his shoulder with his thumb to where the men lay. "They are."

"Sure enough," the bartender said.

Dobkins jabbed Fargo with the derringer again.

"Keep moving, Mr. Fargo," he said.

Fargo kept moving.

No other series has this much historical action!

THE TRAILSMAN

Available wherever books are sold or at
penguin.com

Penguin Group (USA) Online

What will you be reading tomorrow?

Tom Clancy, Patricia Cornwell, W.E.B. Griffin,
Nora Roberts, William Gibson, Robin Cook,
Brian Jacques, Catherine Coulter, Stephen King,
Dean Koontz, Ken Follett, Clive Cussler,
Eric Jerome Dickey, John Sandford,
Terry McMillan, Sue Monk Kidd, Amy Tan,
John Berendt...

You'll find them all at
penguin.com

*Read excerpts and newsletters,
find tour schedules and reading group guides,
and enter contests.*

Subscribe to Penguin Group (USA) newsletters
and get an exclusive inside look
at exciting new titles and the authors you love
long before everyone else does.

PENGUIN GROUP (USA)
us.penguingroup.com